No Love
For The
Wicked

JESSICA CAGE

For my grandmother.

You will live on forever in my heart.

Your legacy will go on.

PROLOGUE

For years, I sat by and watched it happen. Time and time again, they walked down the aisle, forever tied to the person they would spend the rest of their lives with. My friends. Don't get me wrong; I was happy for them. Well, I was as happy as I could be, considering it would never be me. But what was I upset about? This wasn't something any proper Dark Conjurn would desire. This wasn't a thing that my darkened heart should ache over. Of course not, because unlike the friends I'd become aligned with, I was branded, marked from birth to be something that never quite felt like right to me. They were the good girls, and me, well, I was wicked. And as they say, there is no love for the wicked.

CHAPTER

ONE

It was after the fourth marriage proposal that I felt it rising from the depths of my guts; anger, resentment, annoyance. Still, I stood there and smiled and cheered because that's what a good friend does. That was the role I played every time. The good supportive friend. Now, had I done what I wanted to do, taken that ring and shoved it down the throat of my friend's overly muscled beau, well that would have ruined everything. Besides, I was already being watched by every witch in the room.

So how did I, Sierra Grey, Daughter of the Dark, end up chummy with a bunch of light witches? Well, that would be because it wasn't until our fourth year of mastery that they decided which side we were all supposed to be on. They believed delaying this announcement would somehow result in mature responses. It would lead to less infighting. The crazy thing is that everyone seemed to know exactly where they belonged. Everyone naturally migrated to their like-minded peers; everyone except me.

I walked into the testing room, knowing with every bit of my being that I would be a Daughter of the Light. When I came out and saw the ashen mark next to my name, I knew I was wrong, and my world crumbled. I looked to my friends, all wearing their white robes as my shoulders were draped in the heavy black material.

We promised each other that no matter what, we would remain friends. And though at times that proved a difficult thing to do, we kept that promise.

Now, here I was, witnessing the last of my friends gush over a massive rock on her finger as planned rose petals fell from a net and drifted to the marbled floor around the happy couple. And it was so beautiful that I could puke. I didn't vomit, however; I sucked back the taste of bile and stayed just long enough to leave, raising no unnecessary suspicion.

Lucky for me, the pathways to my home were closing soon and getting stuck in the Land of Sunshine and Rainbows, as I liked to call it, was not an ideal plan, especially with all the sappy happy happening. It was the perfect excuse for my running away as Tana wiped away a fresh flow of tears from her face and smiled for more pictures.

Here is some background into my world and reason for my aversion to the display of love that I was just forced to sit through.

I live on a planet called Dynundria. It is nearly a mirror image of Earth. It sits right next to the world in another realm. The people of Dynundria were a mirror image of those of Earth, with one exception. Our possession of magic. We have cousins who live on the planet, they're mostly called witches. They are the descendants of Dynundrians who left our world for a chance at a new life on Earth.

Though Dynundria is populated with various magical beings, Conjurns are the primary species. I'm a witch if you haven't figured that out yet, or more accurately said, I'm a Conjurn of the Dark variety. They split the planet into three sectors, the Light, the Dark, and the Haze. At the northernmost point is the Mastery. The Mastery is where we all go to train and learn to hone our magical talents. When we are near our graduation from Mastery, they announce which side we belong on. Light or Dark.

They give us a choice. Accept the decision or go gray and go to the Haze. The Haze is a neutral land and once you go there; you don't come back. That was an option for me, I suppose, I didn't feel like I belonged to the Dark, but going to the Haze meant I never got to see the people I cared about. It also meant giving up magic. They prohibited the use of magic within the boundaries of the Haze. A life without magic sounded like hell; might as well just go to Earth. I loved magic more than anything else. Light or Dark, there was no way I was giving it up.

The passageways between the Light and the Dark were only open three times a day, and if you missed last call, there was no getting back home. I missed it once and trust me; I learned that day just how accurate it was that I wasn't chosen to be in the Light. Everything was just too bright. The sun was too hot, and the air was too pure. I felt like I was choking on it. I hid in Cara's basement until the next passageway opening. By the time I made it home, I felt sick to my stomach and spent two days in bed.

"Sierra, are you leaving?" Tana called out as I pulled the black coat over the black dress that did little to cover the cleavage that made her mother scoff. No, I didn't like too much color. Yes, I loved freaking out the old judgmental Lights.

"Yes, the passage is closing soon." I turned to Tana, a blue-eyed, blonde goddess sporting her new diamond ring. She wiped away the remnants of her mascara as she approached me.

"Oh shoot," she pretended to pout, but had never mastered the art of acting. "Can't you stay? We have to celebrate!" She held out her hand sporting the new dazzling accessory. "Can you believe it? I'm getting married!"

"I have a lot to get done back home and if I get stuck here, I'm screwed. I love you though. Congrats!" I put on my very best happy friend smile and thanked whoever watched over us, that I would not be named her maid of honor purely based on location and availability, also because it would give her mother a heart attack if I were.

The door to the upscale restaurant slid shut behind me, blocking out the sounds of the party inside, and I sighed with relief. A moment later, that sigh turned into one of annoyance as I remembered that I would have to take the long way back to the barrier. Unfortunately for me, the use of dark magic a no-no in the land of the Light, so I was reduced to using pedestrian methods to make it to the passage. I tapped the call button on the post that stood outside of the restaurant and waited for my ride to show up.

The solar-powered vehicle pulled up just as the music from inside shifted to a slow rhythm. The happy couple would now dance for the first time as a newly engaged pair. I slid into the back of the cab, told the driver my destination, and held back the laughter as he realized that I was a Daughter of the Dark.

The drive was uncomfortable as usual. I swear the Lights thought of us as heathens. The second that they took up in their new homes, they forgot that in Mastery most of us were friends. That we spent years building connections only to have them dismantled when the determinations were final. Very few people held together like I did with my girls. Most accepted their new alignments and never looked back.

Getting out of the car, I tapped my wrist to the pad and paid my fare with magical credits that he would no doubt have to go get exchanged before usage. Dark magic, though valuable, could not be wielded by the Light. Magic worked as a currency; earned and traded for goods and services. The strongest witches had the most power, and they lived the lavish lifestyles. Tana, a moderate witch, had just landed herself one of the most powerful witches in the Light. No, I wasn't envious knowing that in a matter of minutes I would be in the Dark and heading back to my humble beginnings.

The one thing I had going was my status. I wasn't a lowly Conjurn. Of my friends, I was in fact the most powerful on my own. Without their counterparts, their husbands, they were all still barely stronger than when we left Mastery. That was the thing about being a Daughter of the Dark, you didn't have to worry about falling in love. No relationships to build meant nothing to distract you from what really mattered.

The passages were points along the barrier wall between the two sectors that opened up for exactly three minutes each, six times a day. The last one being just before 11 p.m. and it wouldn't open again until nine the next morning. I stood on the platform alone as usual, waiting for the passage to open and wondering how long I would have to perfect my fourth and final sequence of the 'I'm so happy you've found your soul mate, though I will never have one,' faces.

Three low tones announced the passageway's opening and a moment later, the tall gray wall hummed. Above the platform was the black dahlia. The flower marked a point of safe transition. It protected our magic as we passed through the passageways. The barriers were a point of neutrality, so that no one could attack another Conjurn, but it was also found that a thief could easily lift another's magic without a trace. The instillation of the dahlias stopped that from happening.

The wall opened and there were three more chimes. The time was now. Move through the passage or stay in the Light. Usually when headed home, especially on the last call, my journey was solo. Rarely did I see anyone else leaving or entering the Light. This time was different. The sound of my footsteps became echoed by another's. I lifted my eyes from the black stilettos to see the silhouette of a damn mountain of muscle.

The closer he got, the more I saw of this stranger. The poorly hidden beneath a cool gray suit that fit him like a damn glove. No, it was more like paint. If it would just rain at that exact moment, his covering could melt away. I lifted my eyes from the broad chest and shoulders, to see sexy lips curved into a sly grin. Smooth brown skin and dammit, the lightest brown eyes I'd ever witnessed. As if the sun itself was holding up inside of him. And there it was, mixed with a scent of honey and sandalwood… Light.

The party between my thighs slammed to a stop as we passed one another. It pleased me as I glanced down to see that I wasn't the only one aroused in this unfortunate situation. I made it to the other side just in time to turn and see the locs that fell to his ass and bit my bottom lip. How I'd imagined riding a stallion like him, using his locs as the reins. I figured I would just enjoy the view until the door slid shut, but then he turned and looked back.

Our eyes connected as we stood on our respective sides,

and for a moment watched each other. I damn near lost all of my senses. The last set of tones chimed, snapping me back to sense, and the passage slid shut with a mocking sound.

"No, love for the wicked," I muttered to myself, snapped my fingers, glad that I could use my magic again to carry me the rest of the way home. Unfortunately, when I got there, I had a not so welcomed visitor waiting for me.

CHAPTER

TWO

You know that moment when you walk into your home and the weight of the world falls away? I had that, for a hot second, because not two seconds after I'd taken my jacket off, a voice that annoyed my soul like nails across a chalk board screeched from the shadows.

"Welcome home, sister." I could hear it in her voice, the standard judgement with a touch a pity.

"Camille," I sighed and pet Maleficent, my black and gray Maine Coon cat who had seen fitter days. Her pudgy stomach rumbled against my palm as she purred. "What the hell are you doing here, again?"

"How could I not come and visit? I've missed you so." Camille snapped her fingers and the lights popped on. Her massive afro stood atop her head like a dark crown as she left the chair to get to her feet. My sister was beautiful, and she knew it. Her curvy frame matched my own, only her breast were manageable C-cups while I sported a bothersome pair of double Ds. Her eyes were the color of honey and her lips plump and always painted with a fresh coating of matte black lipstick.

"Funny how you always seem to miss me on days when I visit the Light." Maleficent tired of my petting, whined, and walked away from me. "I'm starting to think you're just coming to be nosey. Now would I be wrong in that thought?"

"Oh sister, don't be so paranoid. It's not cute on you." Camille sucked her teeth. "But while we're on the topic, why do you keep torturing yourself? It's ridiculous, you know. You go there and watch them live the life that you can only ever dream about. Us Dark Daughters don't get that fairy tale shit. You already know that."

"They're my friends and we've had this conversation a thousand times over. I would think that by now you'd be tired of sounding like a broken record." I left the front room to enter the kitchen. As expected, my sister followed.

"Yes, you'd think that by now I'd be tired of trying to save you from yourself." She leaned against the door frame and watched me navigate the room. "Look, I know that when you were a little girl you wanted all that stuff; love, marriage, babies who don't grow up to hate your guts. Hell, you didn't even think you were going to be in the Dark. Yet here you are, and you keep going there and reminding yourself of everything you had to give up when you chose to come here."

"Why are you here?" I tapped my finger against the kettle, and it heated the water within. What I needed was a nice cup of tea to settle my bones, and to eliminate the thoughts of the stranger in the passageway.

"I am here with another little message from mother. She wonders why you haven't come to see her."

"I'm sorry," I pointed in the direction of the front entrance to my home. "I don't see her knocking on my door. Why should she expect me to suddenly come crawling to her?"

"You two need to squash this. It's getting old."

"You could always just stop playing messenger and poof," I waved my hands in front of her face, "it's all over."

"Yeah, right, like that'll happen." She headed for the door and stopped to pet Maleficent who hissed at her as she did every time. "Oh, stop it fatty," Camille teased the cat as she continued towards the door.

"Thanks for dropping by."

"Anytime dear one. See you tomorrow." She waved over her shoulder and van shed without touching the doorknob.

"Bright and early," I muttered as the kettle cried out. As the lingering essence of her dissipated, I finally relaxed. The way I should have before she invaded my space uninvited and unwelcome. I fixed my cup of tea in proper order. Honey on the bottom of the cup, hot water next, then dropped in the teabag and headed for the stairs that lead up to my bedroom.

The garments that covered my body melted away as I climbed the stairs and my mind drifted back to the cool brown eyes of the stranger in the passageway. I could feel myself once again becoming aroused by just a thought. Oh, what a thought it was. Dammit if he wasn't a Light! What I wouldn't do to that man. But again, as always, I was reminded by my sister's warning. The same one she'd been giving me since I joined her in the Dark. There's no love for the wicked.

By the time I made it to my bathroom, I was completely naked. As the tub filled and the herbs danced through the air before settling into the warm water, I stood in front of the full-length mirror. This was my ritual which began years ago when I had to take time to love the body I was in. I ran my fingertip up my arm an appreciation for the melanin. I turned to the side and winked at my own ass. It was plump, yet firm. I kissed my fingertips and pressed them to my love handles. They were small pudges that said I was well paid and well fed. To end, I crossed my arms in front of myself cupping my breast and gave each nipple a little flick. Though they were bothersome, and heavy as hell, I appreciated the appeal of them.

After my ritual moment of self-appreciation, my mind went back to the mystery man. I slid into the tub bringing the tea with me and watched as the remaining herbs settled into the bath with me. I loved to make them dance around the room because it somehow made the air seem cleaner. The tea did its job. My body relaxed and the weight of the day melted away replaced by an unusual arousal.

My hand dropped beneath the water and my fingers danced between my legs as the image of him returned. Only this time, the man that approached me wasn't burdened by the layers of fabric. His entire muscular being was revealed to me beneath the moonlight. I stood in place as the breeze brushed across my skin and kissed the tips of my breasts. The sight gifted to me was magnificent. Strong thighs carried a wall of a man to me and soon Mr. Brown eyes was standing in front of me, unmoving himself.

I lifted my hands to touch him, traced the lines of his abs, down to his v-cut and to what I imagined was sized to match the rest of him. I reached down and wrapped my hand around him, smiling as the girth was too big for just one hand. I looked up at those eyes and bit my lip as he moaned deeply each time my hand passed the length of him, squeezing gently on the tip before returning to the base again. His locs fell around his face and down his chest, brushing my arm as his head dropped back beneath the moon.

His hand lifted from his side and I braced myself for the strength of his touch, as I watched his fingers near my pelvis. He grabbed hold of my waist and my core tightened as I was pulled against him. His dick was still held firmly in my hand as he kissed me hungrily. I released him, wrapping my arms around his neck and pulling myself up the mountain. My legs wrapped around his waist and prepared for him to enter.

Just as I felt the tip of his heat pressing against my opening, the sound of glass ripped away the best part. I opened my eyes to see the wicked grin of Maleficent. She looked at me and pointed with her tail to the mess she'd made for me. My teacup was shattered on the bathroom floor. The little jerk had knocked it over.

"Dammit, did I forget to feed you?" She meowed as if annoyed that I'd even asked. Jumped down from the edge of the tub and left the room. "You could have given me like five more minutes you know!" I sighed knowing I would never get that moment in my mind back. Once a good dream was ripped away, trying to dive back into it was always pointless.

I ended my bath, fed the fat cat, and headed to bed. Tomorrow was a big day and I needed my rest. It was time for the Culling and my team would need me alert.

THREE

One green eye with blue flecks. One hazel with red.

This was the reflection I'd always known. My mother was so excited when I was born. Excited and yet afraid because no one knew what it meant. In Dynundria everything that was not standard must also have a greater meaning. Any type of anomaly, a prediction of something greater. They convinced my mother that the oddity of my eye color meant that I would somehow catapult our family and her legacy into the history books. It couldn't have been something as simple as a genetic mutation. My eyes meant that I was marked, destined to do something that had yet to be defined.

That is what she and everyone around her feared. The unknown. Every other marker, as they called it, was known. The Old Ones predicted every marker centuries before their birth and logged in the manifest. Some were told to be trackers. They acted as timestamps in history; just a part of a countdown to a greater occurrence. Others were told to possess substantial power and influence over the times. Not all these predictions were accurate. Like Margaret Bonathine, the blue-haired girl ons. She was born, she lived, and she died. Still, it had been eons since the last reports of dragons. Yet my mother and the rest of the old hags still put their faith in those predictions.

At least most people born with markers or mutations were able to hide them. In most cases it was something insignificant like a birthmark in an odd shape, a weird hair color which could be masked by dye or a wig. My personal favorite was the guy with the odd colored mole. A fucking mole! My mutation appeared right on my face and unable to be hidden, even by magic. I tried everything I could think of, special lensed glasses, contacts, spells, potions and even eye creams. Hell, I was young and dumb and would listen to just about anything someone told me to try. Nothing worked. I just wanted to be normal. I wanted to be able to fade into the background.

It was after my graduation from Mastery that everyone seemed to give up on my mutation. It no longer meant anything other than my parental combination was in some way unique on a genetic level. That marked the beginning of a five-year transition when I was able to, for the most part, slip away into the obscurity. I loved every moment of it. The only time anyone paid any attention to me was when I visited the Light, but in the Dark, I was just your average plain Jane.

That was until three years ago, just after my twenty-fifth birthday. As if it were some kind of delayed joke by the gods of puberty, my body decided once again to betray me. Until that age I had a boyish frame but something hormonal happened. I woke up one day with an ass that wouldn't fit into anything I owned and breasts that announced my arrival five minutes before I entered a room. This created a new attention I wanted to hide from. The kind from those with dangly bits between their thighs.

This brought a fresh new hell to my world. Male attention. Overnight, the world took on the belief that the spread in my hips meant that I should be spreading my legs for anyone interested. The result of course, a new child to feed into the program.

Oddly enough, the need for new children was the reason I had a job working the Culling.

The Culling was a quarterly trip that took my crew and several like us across the barrier to Earth. Once there we were to recruit the strongest of their descendants to bring them back home to Dynundria. This became necessary because of the Conjurns, like me, who chose not to produce offspring. I know the nerve. Here I had the nerve to be knocking on 30 and I had yet to pop out a seed. Granted, I would be fertile for another two-and-a-half centuries, plenty time to bare children. However, our numbers had dwindled by five percent every decade for the last century and a new job needed to be filled. One that I happened to be damn good at. No, I wouldn't produce offspring, but I would gladly go snatch up a couple witches from another realm. It was the highest paying gig a girl could have, and it meant I only had to work a few times a year.

I strapped on my boots, kissed Maleficent goodbye, and headed for the Hull, the hunters' headquarters. That was my job title. Hunter. It sounded so barbaric. We didn't hunt anything. We followed set beacons, had conversations with the target, and tried to convince them to come back with us. If they agreed they came, if not, we wiped their memories of our existence and returned home empty-handed.

The Hull wasn't far from my home, so I chose to stroll through the dull streets under the sky that was always thick with clouds. Always a good idea to clear the mind before entering the Hull. Unfortunately, the Dark differed from the Light for many reasons. Not only was it gloomier on our side of the wall, but it was uglier, and far more depressing. Along the streets were the homeless, begging for any magical credits that could be spared. I couldn't remember ever seeing one homeless person in the Light.

There wasn't much greenery either. The grass was brown and dried out, despite the constant rain. If there was a home with vibrant colors, you could bet your ass that it belonged to a powerful Conjurn. Every time I returned home; the blatant issues were harder to ignore. I began to wonder if my sister wasn't right. My trips to the Light may have become a negative thing for me. Still, I wanted to keep my friends in my life.

I had to take my mind off the inequities that surrounded me. It was time to prepare myself for the onslaught of testosterone that awaited my arrival at the Hull. Most hunters were men. I was one of only three female hunters. My sister and a short-haired vixen named Ramira who kept to herself were the other two. Fresh out of Mastery, I landed the job that no one thought I was qualified for and I worked my ass off every damn day to prove them wrong. Within two years, I earned a rank higher than 90 percent of my sector. A year after that I was named Captain of my own team. Two years later, my team had the highest success rating of all the Hunter crews. Not qualified, my ass!

The short walk down the dreary streets ended too soon. The gates to the Hull buzzed, and I was allowed to walk through. I nodded at the guard who sat bored in the stone tower just beyond the gates. It had been centuries since such security was needed. The most action Richard ever saw was a stray squirrel landing on an electric post. And that only meant a nasty cleanup job for the old guard.

I made my way down the cold stone path, up the steps and into the front door to find my team standing in the lobby wearing frustrated expressions.

"What the hell is going on here?" I took account, everyone was present. "Why aren't you all in briefing?"

"Your guess is as good as ours Captain," a dark-haired, green-eyed, giant of a man who only liked to be referred to as Chaos reported. "We were told to wait here for further instruction."

"Where is Kianna?" Kianna was the Hull's formal secretary and the only person Hunters ever interacted with. All the High Officials worked out of the Hull but when Hunters appeared, they got scarce.

"I'm here, Sierra," Kianna called from the top of the stairs that lead to the second floor. As she descended the steps, a line of faces followed her. Each one unfamiliar, until the last. The lump formed in my stomach as I watched them continue to approach us. The smell reached our group before they did. The scent of sunshine, rainbows, and Light.

"Since when are Lights allowed inside the Hull?" Camille stepped to my side as she questioned Kianna's guests.

"Since we've had a change of plans from above," the secretary responded unbothered. "If you have any concerns, feel free to fill out a form." She pointed to the dust-covered desk at the center of the room. On it sat a single black pen, a pad of complaint forms, and a box that remained untouched since it the decorator put there.

"Change of plans?" I questioned Kianna in leu of allowing my mind to race over the man who'd invaded my dreams the night before. "What are the new plans? Are we not going on this Culling?"

"Oh, you're going. It would seem that our population issues are now affecting those of the Light as well as the Dark. Because of this, Mr. Maxwell and his team will be joining team Grey on your next Culling tour. Your trip will also be delayed by one day so that we can make sure that everyone is aligned on the goals of this excursion."

"Great," Chaos muttered under his breath.

"Oh, chill out, big boy. Are you in a rush to come up empty again?" Ramira, who'd been quietly observing, slapped Chaos on the arm. "You'll get your chance to get out there."

"I told you," Chaos started in on the same explanation of his last failed recruitment. A saucy brunette who mesmerized him with her wide eyes and full lips and slipped away. Ramira was there to intercept her before she could tell anyone about her interaction with Chaos. She wiped the brunette's memory.

"Yea yeah, keep the excuses." Ramira laughed. "Bright eyes and a fat ass knocked you off your game. Plain and simple."

"Ms. Grey," Kianna interrupted the spat between two members of my team. "As the head of your team, you will stay here for further briefing. The rest of you return tomorrow bright and early for assignments and launch. I need Ms. Grey and Mr. Maxwell in the debriefing room." Without a further word, she turned and headed back up the stairs.

"Okay team, you heard her." When I turned to address

them, I made a point to ignore the raised brow of my sister. There would be plenty of time to dish later.

"Great, a day off!" Ramira slapped her hand against Milo's. He was the smallest member of our team. He dressed in muted tones and never spoke, which was why Ramira liked him.

"I'll speak to you later," Camille commented as I turned on my heals and headed to debriefing.

CHAPTER
FOUR

The debriefing room was a sterile white space with one large table and about twenty chairs. A large window overlooked the courtyard where one tree stood surrounded by dead grass. Luckily, I made it there before my counterpart and oddly before Kianna, which was a relief. I needed the time to myself, to wrap my head around the surprise of seeing him there. This man was supposed to be a missed connection that I fantasized about for a few weeks. Instead, he turned into a nightmare that followed me to work. I had to compose myself. If Kianna picked up on even a hint of sexual tension between the two of us, she'd be reporting our asses.

Light and the Dark Conjurns could not get busy. Yeah, we could be friends, visit each other's territories, but that was it. None of the fun stuff. Definitely none of the things I dreamt about doing to Mr. Maxwell the night before.

The door swung open, and he walked through. Just as he was the night before, Mr. Maxwell was dressed in the gray suit, his hair pulled back into a low bun at the base of his neck. He nodded at me and took a seat. Perhaps it wouldn't be an issue. It didn't seem as if he were at all as interested in me as I'd thought. Sitting on the opposite side of the table, I tried not to appear as disappointed as I felt.

"Your eyes really are like that." He tilted his head to the side as he stared into my eyes.

The sound of his voice caught me by surprise and it took my mind a moment to reply, "Excuse me?"

"I thought it was an effect of the passageway, or maybe I was just tired from the events of the day but," he leaned closer to me, "one green eye, one hazel."

"Yes, and?" I straightened my shoulders, preparing for the same flood of questions that everyone always had, which ended in asking me what the colors meant.

Instead of pummeling me with questions, he said two words that left me with no retort, "It's... interesting."

"Okay," Kianna entered the room. The sound of her stiletto pumps broke the silence and interrupted the awkward moment. "Let's make this quick, I have a spa date and was supposed to be out of here an hour ago. As I stated previously, you two are going to be working together. Goal is the same as usual, bring back the assigned descendants. We need to replenish our numbers. Only this time, the two of you will break away from your teams."

"What do you mean we will break away?"

"There is something more that needs to come back from Earth. We're trusting this to the two of you." She dropped two packets on the table between us.

"What is it?" He picked up his packet and fingered through the provided documents.

"A seed," Kianna answered.

"A seed?" I laughed dryly. We'd gotten some odd requests in the past, requests for food, drinks, even clothing, but nothing like this. "You want us to abandon the mission to bring back a seed?"

"This is above me. I'm just reporting the orders, and I've been told that this is highly important, so I suggest you two not fuck it up. Everything you need to know is in the packets. If you have any further questions, ask each other." Kianna rolled her eyes and left us in the room alone.

"Well, that was informative." He leaned back in his seat and looked at the door that Kianna had made her exaggerated exit through.

"We should begin reading." I opened my packet. "Usually, I would do this alone at home, but I'd like to make sure we're on the same page before we leave here today."

"Sounds good to me. So, we're hunting for a seed."

"Says here it's an origin seed."

"An Origin Seed? Are you sure?" he stood up to move around the table and looked at the document over my shoulder. I had to hold my breath to steady myself as he did. "I've only read about these. Origin seeds only appear when a major historic event is about to happen."

His breath brushed across my cheek as he spoke, and I pressed my thighs tighter together before responding. "It must be something they're afraid of. Why else would they have us going after this in such a secretive way? As far as I remember, the last time an Origin Seed formed, all of Dynundria celebrated. Why the concealment now?" I spread the pages out on the table in front of me and picked up the sheet that detailed the location. "Oh great, it's at the mouth of a damn volcano. They couldn't make it easy, could they?"

"Well, that's why they chose the best for the job." He pulled out the chair next to mine and sat. "I've read your file. You've had an impressive career in such a short time."

"Thanks, I would return the compliment but I know nothing about you Mr. Maxwell."

"Horacio." He smiled. "You can call me Horacio."

"Horacio." I nodded. "I suppose I can get to know you on our journey tomorrow."

"Yes, that sounds like a plan."

"This all looks cut and dry." I peered over the documents again. "Outside of our deviation, the teams will have a standard list of descendants to recruit. This list was a little lengthier than usual, but that's why your team is here. I figure we can match one of your guys with one of mine. They're more experienced and we can use this as a training opportunity. How does that sound to you?"

"Sounds like a solid plan. I will relay the information to my team tonight." He chuckled and his shoulders shook. "I can just imagine the response I'm going to get to this."

"Yeah, I know. Ramira will not be pleased with being paired with a Light."

We spent the next three hours reviewing the documents and going over the pairs that would work together. Selecting members from my team to work with him proved a difficult task. The hardest to match was Milo, but we created assignments that would be the least disastrous.

By the end of our meeting, we were laughing and joking like old friends. He wasn't like the other men of the Light. They were stuffy, conceited, and looked down on anyone from the

Dark. It came from years of being told that they were the counterpart to our evil. They were good, and that meant that they were better than we were.

Horacio wasn't like that. I never felt like he thought I didn't earn my place at the table beside him. He listened to my ideas instead of telling me what they should have been. His maturity and humility made him even sexier in my eyes. By the time we finished the task at hand, I was so wet between the legs I feared he could smell my arousal.

He laughed at a joke I couldn't remember telling and in an attempt to place his hand on my shoulder; he missed and his hand landed on my left breast. My eyes dropped to his hand, which lingered there longer than it should have.

"Oh, I am so sorry," he said staring at his hand then up to me.

"It's okay." I looked down at his hand still resting on my chest. "You done?"

"Shit," he pulled his hand back, and I held in the urge to laugh at his embarrassment.

"How about we call it a day?" I suggested and began gathering the pages to avoid glancing down to see if his arousal was as obvious as my own.

"Yes, we should do that. I must meet with my team and we should all rest up. Big trip tomorrow." That was the first time I'd seen him look nervous. It was nice, knowing that it wasn't just me.

"Yes," I stood. "You wouldn't want to miss your passageway and get stuck on our side of town."

"We'll be bunking here tonight. We'll be leaving early. Not enough time to make it here and get prepared before launch."

"Right, well, see you tomorrow." I arranged the documents in the sleeve, tucked it under my arm, and head for the door.

"Sierra," his smooth voice brushed against the back of my mind and stopped me before I could make it to the door. I took a deep breath and turned to face him again.

"Yes?" I looked over my shoulder to the man who focused on the task at hand.

"I like your eyes," he said without looking up from his own stack of documents.

"Um, thanks," I forced my voice to form the response before turning back to the door and leaving. I had to get the hell out of there or I might have risked it all.

The dream that night was more intense than I'd experienced before. If I hadn't woken up in my sweat drenched bed, I might have been convinced that it was more reality than dream. I was so bothered by the images that played on a highlight reel in my mind that looking Horacio in the eye the next day proved difficult. Still, I managed to stand beside him as we received our official assignments and loaded into the pods that would carry us across the barrier wall to Earth.

CHAPTER
FIVE

"Sister," Camille stepped in front of me, pretending to adjust the belts of the backpack. Her voice lowered to a barely audible whisper, "be careful."

"What are you talking about?" I took account of our surroundings, making note of any pending threat. Could she see something that I couldn't?

"We're safe for now. I see how you look at Mr. Hot Stuff over there," she nodded her head slightly towards Horacio. "That's a dangerous game."

"Camille, I—"

"Look, I'm just looking out for you." Camille looked at me with eyes like I'd never seen on my sister. She was worried. More than that, she looked afraid. "You're toying with trouble. You know the rules."

"The rules are stupid," I joked to take the edge off the moment. "Besides, I haven't done anything wrong and don't plan on it."

"I'm not saying I disagree with you; some rules were definitely made to be broken. I don't want you to end up locked away because you finally choose someone to play with and he's from the wrong side of the fence."

"I haven't chosen to do anything. You're overreacting." Kianna's footsteps sounded off her approach. "Drop it, please."

"You remember that when we get to Earth and the two of you are all alone in that jungle heat."

"Camille." If she continued, no matter how much she lowered her tone, Kianna's nosey ass would overhear. That would only cause me trouble I hadn't earned.

"I know, shut it. Whatever." She tugged at my straps one final time and shot a glance in Horacio's direction. "Don't say I didn't warn you."

The teams loaded up into the pod that would serve as our portal. The oval-shaped compartment would be sent across space and time by the Conductor. The Conductor was a massive contraption that used the forces of nature to build energy. Once a quarter, each Conductor would store enough energy to power exactly one twelve-hour trip. After that it would shutdown and the pod would be pulled back to Dynundria. If you weren't on the pod at the time of the pullback, you would be stuck on Earth until the next Culling.

The trip was smooth for those of us who were used to it. I read up on Horacio's team. Not one of them had ever taken the trip to Earth. They'd likely been through simulations, but that was nothing like the real thing. The landing was rocky. And before we could unstrap our safety harnesses, Stephen, the Lights counterpart chosen to work with Chaos, hurled all over Ramira's shoes. I had to applaud her restraint. Istead of attacking the green-faced man, she shot me a hot glare.

"So, this is Earth?" Paula, one of the Lights, frowned her face as she stepped out of the pod that had landed in a cornfield. All over the world, there were farmlands run by Dynundrians that provided us safe passage to and from Earth. Still the pod set invisible to the naked eye. "It stinks here."

"Air pollution. The human population has no regard for the planet." Ramira looked down at her feet with a grimace. "Like your buddy had for my shoes."

"Sorry about that." Stephen still held his hand on his stomach as he tried to settle the motion within.

"Alright, listen up," I took command, "we all have our assignments. You know who your buddies are. Stay hidden, move quickly, leave no evidence of our being here. Remember, no one can know about us. Lock in the coordinates of this location. We have twelve hours to do this. That's not a lot of time to convince someone to walk away from their entire life. There is no time for sightseeing."

"Yes, ma'am." Chaos grinned and placed his hand on Paula's shoulder. "Let's go, Missy. I'd like to get this over with." He waved his hand in the air, drawing the symbol of transport which opened a portal to take them to their destination. The two crossed the portal and vanished from the field.

Milo and Stephen were next to leave, followed by Ramira and Kyler, an equally spunky woman who wouldn't let Ramira walk over her. Camille was last to leave. She stood there with her partner for the day, a man name Jack with a mole the size of a peanut that sat on his left cheek. I could just imagine the commentary my sister would provide when this job was done.

Before launching their portal, Camille pulled me to the side to issue her final warning. "Remember what I said."

"Camille, I'm a professional," I reminded her. "I can handle myself. He isn't the first attractive man I've worked with."

"So, you find him attractive?" she teased.

"Hell, I'm professional, not blind! Go, you're wasting time."

"Alright, I'm all set." She called out to her partner before she opened the portal, "Come on hot stuff."

"So, that's your sister." He watched the portal close.

"Yes, aren't I so lucky?" I laughed and adjusted my backpack. "You want to do the honors or shall I?"

"Allow me," his hands moved skillfully to create the portal that would take us to our location. He came with a team composed of novices, but Horacio was not one.

We stepped through the portal transporting from a cornfield in the countryside of the Americas to New Zealand's North Island. The soil beneath our feet was formed from volcanic ash. This made it highly fertile, and the perfect location for an Origin Seed to grow. Our directives state that we would find the seed near Mt Tongariro, a volcano which hadn't erupted in nearly eight years, but I didn't trust it.

Horacio's portaling proved to be accurate as we stepped right at the base of the Tongariro Crossing, a path that many people came to hike. Luckily, we didn't land in the middle of a group of tourist.

The temperature around the volcano was warmer than I was used to, still I managed. With a few adjustments to my outfit, I was able to cool off. My magic worked on Earth as well as it did on Dynundria. I swapped out the black cargo pants for shorts and the jacket for a tank top.

"This should be easy enough. Based on this map, we have about an eight-hour hike up and then back down. But I created these special shoes, with them we should be able to do it in half the time." He opened his backpack and handed me a pair of hiking boots that were far from stylish. "They'll also make sure that we remain hidden from the human eye. We wouldn't want to break the most important rule."

"Hike? We have to climb this thing?" I looked up the elevation to the summit of Tongariro. "Great. So, I'm assuming magic is a no go here."

"Yes, the details in our packet states that there are properties in the ash that will disrupt any portal we try to create to get closer." He adjusted his attire as well. Long sleeves were removed to show his arms, and his pants shifted to shorts. I managed to keep my eyes focused on safe zones like his face, the sky, or the mountain range. "If we open a portal to try to get to the top, we could end up in the rain forest somewhere. The shoes will help us gain speed, but that's as good as I could do."

"Wonderful." I put the shoes on and wiggled my toes as they formed to my feet. "You're real handy to have around."

"Thanks." He put his own on, then stretched his legs to prepare for the hike. "You ready to do this?"

"Ready as I'll ever be."

The shoes gave the sensation of running across water. The ground gave us little resistance. The technology he built caused the surface to be dispersed by our weight. Each step sent us further ahead than the one before it. It took a bit to get used to, but once I did, it was easy going.

"Suppose we could make small talk to pass the time?" I suggested three hours into an awkward hike where we'd only made comments on the surrounding wildlife and vegetation.

"What would you like to talk about?" He navigated the terrain effortlessly, while keeping a constant check on our perimeter. I was impressed. Part of me expected him to be a wimp considering he was a Light.

"How about we discuss why the hell they have us searching for the Origin Seed instead of more of the descendants?" I kept pace with him as we began our conversation. "Any scout could have done this, it's not at all a difficult task, yet they choose the best of the best to do this. Something about that just doesn't add up to me."

"I've been wondering about that as well, but I suppose they wouldn't have us out here if it weren't important."

"The leaders of the Light gave you no further insight?" I pried. The Dark would never tell me a thing that they didn't think I needed to know, no matter how much I questioned them. Maybe things were different on his side of the world.

"I was told," he paused and continued in an almost robotic manner, "It is of great importance to the future of Dynundria."

"Yeah, same here. Blanket statement bullshit." I stopped and waited for him to realize that I was no longer behind him.

"Are you okay?" He returned to me, sweat beading on his forehead. "Did you hurt yourself?"

"Do you believe the bullshit?"

"What?" Still he examined me with his eyes, looking for an open wound.

"I need to know what kind of man you are. Do you buy into the shit they're shoveling us about this mission?" I sipped from the canteen of water, allowing my temperature to cool as I waited for him. The sun was bearing down from above, and dammit if it didn't feel like the ground was heating up too. If this was the day, the damned volcano decided to become active again, I would be kicking some major ass when I got home.

"You're really blunt, aren't you?"

"Should I be any other way?" I winked at him as I wiped

om my lips. "I'm a Daughter of the Dark, after all."

"I suppose you are." He held out his hand for the water and I shared it. After he took a long sip, he continued. "No, I don't believe it. I find it suspicious, just like you do. But I'd never been to Earth before. I wanted to see what it was like. Hell, it shocked me when they gave me the assignment for this mission, considering my life at home is more about being in the lab. I keep fit, but I'm not someone who is traversing up the side of a volcano."

"You're here out of a thirst for adventure, not out of blind obedience. I can get with that." I adjusted the straps of my backpack and moved past him to continue the hike.

"What if I would have given a different answer?" his voice called from behind me.

"Well then Mr. Maxwell," I turned to him, "there may have been an unfortunate accident for you."

"Very funny."

The heat at the bottom of my feet continued to grow. "Are these things supposed to get so hot?"

"Hot?"

"It feels like I'm standing on an oven."

"That's not good." He knelt down to look at his handy uppose I should have tested them at a longer rate of time."

"What are you trying to say? These things are going to cook my feet?"

"I don't know." The look he gave me caused heat traveled up my leg to tickle the special spot between my thighs. "We better hurry up, just in case."

"Right, kick it into high gear and hope I can still wear my stilettos later."

CHAPTER

SIX

We kept up the conversation as we rushed to finish the rest of our hike. I wanted to know more about Horacio and judging by the battery of questions he had in response to my own; the feeling was mutual. We discussed all the ways our lives differed on different sides of the wall. Covering topics from work, to family, even relationships, which neither of us had many of. Getting to know him was great, but I realized too late how dangerous a practice it was. I could hear Camille in the back of my mind yelling at me with each bit of information I offered.

"There it is." Horacio stopped and pointed. A few yards ahead of us was a solitary plant, perched on the side of the volcanic mouth. There were people all around us, but we remained invisible.

"Awesome, I can take these damn things off now." I activated the shield attached to my backpack to keep me hidden from the tourists who rested before their hike back down before I reached down and ripped the boots off my feet. Before the damned things hit the ground, my feet had cooled to a tolerable temperature despite where I was standing. If my magic were working, my feet would have been in an ice bath.

"We just have to get the seed out of the pod and we're good to go." Horacio dropped to his knees and began searching for the containment vessel that they gave us to transport the seed.

While he searched, I moved closer to the plant. It was beautiful. Black vines lifted from the group to meet dark violet petals that folded in on each other. As I neared it, the petals relaxed and bloom, opening wide enough for me to see the crimson-colored seed. The thing was about the size of my palm and my hand was itching. Despite the protocol I'd read and memorized the night before, I couldn't help myself. I felt drawn to it.

Under no circumstance were we supposed to touch it. It was clear. Use the tongs to pick up the seed, place it inside the containment vessel. In big bold letters: NO PHYSICAL CON-TACT. Something inside me, I suppose it was that wickedness everyone was so worried about, said fuck that piece of paper! I reached out and plucked the seed from the core of the flower. The petals turned black and then to ash.

"Wait, did you forget that they said not to touch it?" Horacio's voice was a cool echo in the back of my mind that lin-gered as it flooded my head with thoughts that were not my own. Sights, sounds, sensations that overloaded my senses. SEX. A surge of hormones washed over me.

It was too late for his warning and too late for my senses. What felt like a gentle vibration turned into heat. Not the kind that made my skin sweat, but the kind that induced a different moisture; between my legs.

I turned on him. Dropped the seed to the ground at my feet and undressed.

"What are you doing?" Holding the tongs in his hand, he

knelt down to pick up the seed and place in inside the vessel. When he completed his task, his eyes found my fully exposed form standing in front of him.

"What I've wanted to do since I first saw you." My finger touched his chin, lifting him from his knees. His eyes widened as he stood.

"This isn't right." His lips protested, but his eyes were glued to my breasts. "Light and dark are not to mix."

"Well, those are rules for Dynundria." I clutched his belt buckle in my hand and pulled his waist to mine. "Tell me, Mr. Maxwell, are we on Dynundria now?"

"No, I suppose we aren't." He swallowed as his shorts fell and I draped the belt around his neck.

"Then I don't see a problem here." My hand slid beneath the band of his boxers to find his arousal. The corners of my lips lifted as I found he was just as I expected. Long and girthy.

"Sierra," his eyes closed and head fell back as my hand stroked the length of him.

"Horacio," I responded.

"We shouldn't be doing this."

"And yet," I continued stroking him and felt him grow longer. "Something tells me you want it just as much as I do."

"We could get in trouble."

"I won't tell if you won't." My lips pressed against his neck before my tongue drew a line up to the base of his chin. Even his sweat was an aphrodisiac.

"I—"

I put my finger over his lips. "No more talking, Mr. Maxwell." My lips replaced my finger.

It must have been the taste of me. Once our lips met, all

39

his inhibitions ceased to exist. His hands traveled every curve of my body, cupping my ass and breast simultaneously. He lifted me from the ground and wrapped my legs around his waist. I moaned as his mouth wrapped around my nipple, sucking and teasing with his teeth. His fingers found my pussy and within moments were coated in my juices.

"Dammit," he growled.

"Horacio."

"Yes, Sierra?"

"I want you inside me." I looked him in the eye. "Right now."

"Fuck," he growled again, this time in a primitive nature as he reached down and gave me what I wanted. The tip of him pressed against me for a moment as my opening stretched to fit him. The length of him entered me and we fucked right there, surrounded by unknown humans. I cried out his name as waves of orgasm rushed over me.

He lowered me from his waist, turned me around and entered me again. My body trembled as he filled me from behind. His hands reached around me, and he grabbed my breasts, teasing my nipples between his fingers.

"I'm coming."

"Don't you dare." I pulled away from him. Turned around and pushed him onto the ground. As I gripped the base of his dick and rode him. "You get to cum when I say so."

"Fuck!" His fingers dug into my thighs as I continued to slide up and down, my pussy tightening with each thrust.

Just as I felt myself climbing to the climax, I released him and he grabbed my waist, driving himself deeper into me. I collapsed, sweat drenched and satisfied on top of him.

"That was," he panted.

"Fun," I finished his sentence with a wicked flare. "Let's do it again."

"As much as I would love to, we have to get back." He kissed my neck and grabbed my ass.

"Yes, I suppose we do." I sat up, legs still straddling him, and looked down at those dark eyes that watched my breast. Horacio was definitely a boob guy. "I guess I should get from on top of you."

"That would be helpful." He lifted from the ground to kiss my nipples.

"Mr. Maxwell, that isn't fair."

"Ms. Grey, I didn't think you'd mind."

A few minutes later we were both dressed, hydrated and ready to head back to the pod. Luckily, we could use a portal to leave. If we missed our target, correcting our course would be easy enough. We'd still make it back before the others and could hide what we'd done. His ingenious shoes would not be an option for us, I would not risk losing a foot to save a few hours.

Horacio finished securing the Origin Seed in the vessel, and once the seal was in place, the seductress I'd become left as quickly as she appeared, and I was aware of the gravity of our actions. I could see the same moment of clarity play on his face. This man had seen me bare; he'd seen my love handles and the mole on my right breast, and he didn't give one damn. As he opened the portal, my mind shifted elsewhere. All I could think about was that in a matter of hours I would have to face my sister who, despite my attempt to clean myself up, would have no trouble smelling the sex on me.

CHAPTER

SEVEN

"You ever going to come clean about what happened?" Camille waited for me inside my house.

"Must you always pop up in my space uninvited?" Exhaustion crept from the tips of the toes to the top of my head. Combine the events of the day's trip and the grueling reports Kianna insisted I complete before coming home, and my body was ready to collapse. The second we were back in Dynundria, she bombarded Horacio and I, took the Origin Seed and handed us paperwork to fill out. The policy stated that I had a week to turn in reports, but for reasons unknown to me, that wasn't the case this time around.

They forced me to sit across from Horacio going over the details of the excursion, all while trying not to think about the taste of the sweat on his skin, or the flick of his tongue across my nipples. We completed our reports and review the recounts of our teams with just enough time for him to make the final passageway back to the Light.

What a fucking relief that was. I don't think I would have been able to think straight knowing that he was still in the Dark and that I could straddle him with a snap of my fingers. At least the border would stop me from fucking him and myself.

"Oh please, if you didn't want me to do it, you would have warded the house by now to stop me. So, dear sister, answer my question." Camille stood by the doorway to the kitchen and tapped her foot as she waited for me to address her.

"I don't know what you're talking about." I wasn't going to just come out and tell her I'd ridden Horacio like a stallion in the middle of a crowd of tourist.

"Sure, you do not understand what I'm talking about, but I can sense it on you." She came closer and took a creepy ass deep breath. "I can smell him on you. Don't tell me what you did, fine, but be sure you don't let anyone else find out either. I would hate to see my little sister shipped off to the Haze because she had trouble keeping it in her pants."

"What is it?"

"Your pussy!" She snickered and then vanished.

"That woman needs help," I said as Maleficent moaned. "Yeah, yeah. I'll feed you. I swear you're about as bad as she is."

By the time I made it to my bed, my body was heavier than ever before. The effects of running at hyper speed in those boots had kicked in and my legs cramped. I worked an age-old spell, moving the air around my body to massage the aches away.

I sunk into the mattress and thanked the stars that I wouldn't have to get up to perform any duties the next day. At least all my reports and responsibilities were complete at the Hull. Kianna wouldn't be bothering me again for at least a week when we began plotting for the next Culling. My mind eased along with the aches in my body and I drifted away, expecting to relive the moments of our time on the side of a volcano. Instead, I found myself thrust into what would be a unique experience.

Instead of Mt Tongariro, I found myself in a bedroom with a view of one capital city of the Light. The massive bed sat in the center of the minimalist space. Gray walls met a floor colored with dark tones that were hypnotic. The aroma, the room was full of his scent. Deep tones of honey and oak with an edge of something metallic. I couldn't place it, but I loved it.

"Sierra, what are you doing here?" I turned to see him standing in the doorway. He wore the same clothing, and he looked as tired as I felt before I laid in bed.

"Well, this isn't how this dream usually goes."

"Dream?" He waved his hand and thick curtains covered the large paned windows. The small lamp in the corner provided the only light in the room.

"Yes. You're a dream." I crossed the room and met him at the foot of his massive bed. "Dreams of you are so much fun." I kissed his neck.

"You've been dreaming about me?" His hands gripped my waist, pushing me back.

I didn't notice it before, but there was fear in his eyes. He was worried that they would catch us. "Wait, you mean?" I stepped back from him. "This isn't a dream?"

"No, it's not a dream, Sierra. You're in my bedroom." It wasn't until his eyes dropped that I realized I wasn't dressed. "This is very dangerous. Do you know what will happen to us if anyone finds out about this?"

"Shit. How is this possible?" I retraced my steps but couldn't remember doing anything out of the ordinary. As far as I was concerned, I was still in my bed being massaged by the air currents. "I didn't do this."

"You may not know how you did it, but it would seem your subconscious is reaching out to me." His voice took on a clinical quality as he tried to understand the problem at hand. "The only thing I can't understand is how I'm able to feel you here. I've seen projections before but this, this is something." His hand lifted to cup my breast. He flicked my nipple with his thumb. "Can you feel that?"

"Yes, I can." I bit my lip. "That shouldn't be possible, Horacio. My magic shouldn't be able to reach across the wall. I need to figure out how to get back, but dammit, I don't even know how I got here."

"I agree. This is a conundrum. You shouldn't be here, and yet here you are." He stepped closer and with a slight move of his hand, discarded his clothing. He dropped to his knees in front of me and cupped my ass in his hands.

"What are you doing?" I looked down at him.

"I can't help it. You're intoxicating woman." He looked up at me and his locs fell to the side of his face. "I didn't get to taste you."

"What?"

"He grabbed my right leg and draped it over his shoulder before his lips disappeared between my thighs. Had it not been for the grip I had on his shoulders, I would have fallen over. My body trembled from the pleasure. His tongue was like a magic wand all on its on, I swear the damn thing vibrated! Without ceasing his consumption of me, he lifted me from the ground and laid me on the bed.

"Damn, you're amazing at that." I gripped the sheets as a wave of ecstasy released from my core and sent tingles to my toes. His lips left my clit, leaving me disappointed until they

46

found my nipple. He simultaneously teased me with his teeth and entered me. The ache was only momentary as I stretched once again to fit him.

I let him have his way with me from every direction he could think of until we both collapsed on the bed, covered in sweat and unable to move. He pulled me into him, my back against his chest. The weight of his arm draped across my stomach was like a security blanket. I scoffed as the taste of girly emotions bubbled up inside of me and I had to check myself and shut that shit back down. This wasn't something I could get comfortable with.

"We can't keep doing this. Not here." I reached down and pulled the sheet over my legs, but gave up when it snagged on something out of view. The chilled air brushed across my sweat drenched flesh. He helped me and covered the rest of my body.

"I agree, but if you plan on continuing to appear in front of me with no clothing on," he growled into my ear and nibbled on my lobe. "I can't promise that it won't happen again."

"You need to have a stronger will power, Mr. Maxwell."

"Yeah, sexy naked woman in my bedroom. Will power." He kissed my shoulders and tightened his hold around my waist. "What's that?"

"Work on it. I can't promise this won't happen again." I laughed through a yawn as exhaustion took over. "Hell, I'm not even sure how it happened this time."

"Yeah, I'll do that." As my body relaxed against him, the magic faded and I slowly disappeared from his bed. Whatever magic I'd worked to get me there was fading. Just before I was home again in my bed, I heard him whisper, "See you around, Ms. Grey."

Fuck. I was in trouble.

EIGHT

Two days later I'd managed not to mind fuck Horacio again. It helped that I didn't know how I did it the first time around. I'd be lying if I said I didn't ponder the mechanics behind it. For two days I remained inside the confines of the Dark, but the time had come for me to visit the Light again. I waited for the passageway to open and take me to the other side. I had to go there for the first of six of the Light ritual parties that took place before the actual marriage. Yes. six. I sighed and got my mind ready to cheer for my friend.

On the way to the gathering, I kept reminding myself that until that fateful night, I'd never seen Horacio before. We'd never cross paths. Trust me, I would have remembered it if we did. There was nothing to worry about. The event was being held at a restaurant I'd been to countless times before. It was a favorite of my friends for hosting big events. I would just have to keep my head down, go straight there and straight back. Simple enough.

I was so preoccupied by my thoughts I forgot to take pleasure in making the driver of the transport uncomfortable. I paid my fare and headed into the restaurant. It was still early; I could stay long enough to catch the next passageway home. My mind was hard at work planning excuses for missing a few of the gatherings. She didn't need me to be there for everything. The fewer times I went to Light, the less likely it was for me to bump into him.

The man was on my mind so much that I could smell him. As the door opened to the building, the aroma of him welcomed me and my pussy quivered. "Get it together!" I muttered to myself as I handed my coat over to the attendant.

The event was typical. Awkward reintroductions to Lights who acted as if they'd never seen me before, followed by a decent enough meal, speeches from the key family members and then phase one of their bonding. The process comprised five phases during which would bond the couple on every level possible. From the physical to the mental parts of their body. The process of marriage for Dynundrians was one that should last forever.

First was the marriage of their minds. In this, they could understand how the other processed thoughts and literal things. Then there was the physical marriage, any pain one mate endured, the other would feel. After the physical bond came the emotional connection. They did this one in private as it made the pair vulnerable for about a week, but it was important for a deeper understanding of the person they were to bonded to forever. The next step was when their magic would merge. They would be stronger when together, which would increase their earning potential. The last phase was the spiritual bonding. They did this in a lavish show as their spirits would lift from their physical selves and intertwine, leaving traces of themselves on the other before settling back into their body.

As the happy couple entered the Private chamber tucked away at the back of the banquet hall to begin the first phase, the music started and the awkward socializing kicked off. This was my cue to find a corner to hide in until my friend emerged. I would congratulate her, take a few pictures for memories and then make it back to the passageway. My other friends were busy with their husbands and had forgotten about my existence all together. This was becoming a trend I found somewhat unsettling. I felt like a satellite, stuck in their orbit, close enough to see what was happening but not enough to be a part of any of it.

As I stared out the window at the night sky I caught it again, his scent. Just as I was preparing to sign myself up for a psych evaluation, sound accompanied smell. "First you're in my dreams, now you're in my restaurant."

"Mr. Maxwell," I spoke his name without turning from the window.

"Ms. Grey." His voice lowered as he said my name and I could feel his arousal, though there was no physical contact between us. Now I'd foud men attractive before. Dynundria has some damn fine men, but this was on a new level. This man didn't even have to be in the same room with me, just the thought of him had my panties soaked and my heart racing. This shit was insane.

"What are you doing here?" I took several deep breaths to clear my mind of the conflicting thoughts inspired by the hormonal surge his presence caused.

"I own this establishment." He sat in the chair next to me and reached down to grab my knees. In one swift movement he turned me in my seat so I was no longer looking up at the blanket of the night sky but into the deep brown pools of his eyes.

"And you crash the parties hosted here?" I struggled to remain composed instead of attacking him like an animal in heat.

"Not at all, just popping in to check to make sure everything is running smoothly. "He smiled and my heart skipped a beat. That was new. "It's my duty as the owner."

"Funny, I've been here more times than I can count, but I don't remember seeing you here checking in on things before."

"That may be because it hasn't been long since gained this establishment. It used to be owned by my uncle."

"I see." I turned from him just enough to retrieve my drink from the table to relive my sudden onset of intense thirst. The wine inside was not enough to satisfy my need.

"Why are you hiding back here in the corner?" he asked as I sat the glass back on the table.

"Well I'm not a fan favorite around these parts." I nodded towards the old woman who was eyeballing me as she whispered in her friend's ear. He followed my eyes and laughed as the woman turned to walk away. "I'm sure they're not happy that you're talking to me now."

"Who cares."

"Well, I'm sure every eligible woman here cares. It doesn't seem to me you've chosen a mate yet. So, they may have been hoping that Mr. Tall, dark and handsome would give them a moment of his time."

"Hmm, tall, dark and handsome, huh?" He flashed a cocky smile. "Well, would you look at that, my time is all booked up."

"Is it now?"

"Yes," he scanned the room, noting all the eyes that were tracking our movements and our intimate conversation. He leaned in close to me to whisper in my ear to add a touch of petty to the moment, which only made him sexier to me. I loved pissing off the snotty Lights. "How about we go for a walk so we can talk and give them something more to gossip about?"

"Oh, how I love to entertain the masses." I winked, glancing over my shoulder at the older woman who scoffed at me.

He stood and held his hand out, helping me from my chair, then rested my hand on the nook of his elbow as he led me out of the door. It was damn near impossible to keep a straight face as everyone we walked by looked at us with eyes that were about to dislodge from their sockets.

I followed his lead up the back steps that led to the rooftop. The sky danced in twisting shades of dark blue, magenta, and deep purples. That was always the sky in Dynundria. Every night we got the magical display full of stars. I'd spent one night on Earth before and if I had to choose between the two, there was no contest. The rooftop was decorated with star lights and encased in glass that would make even the rainiest of nights enchanting.

"So, what did you want to talk about?" I asked as I pulled my eyes from the night sky. The Light had a much better view than the Dark. There were never as many clouds covering the area.

"Have you felt any different since that mission?" There it was again, the clinical side of Mr. Maxwell. For a moment he looked at me like I was an experiment.

"Different in what way?" Yes, I felt different, but I wanted to hear what he had to say first.

"Well, I've had urges that I haven't ever experienced before." He lowered his voice, afraid of being overheard. "Desires that seem to drown out every other thing in my life."

"Desires for?"

"You, Ms. Grey."

"Oh."

"Yes. And until recent events, that has never been an important thing in my life. Nothing was ever of greater concern than my work. I'm not a blind man, Sierra. I see the beauty that surrounds me. Still, I felt numb to it. Now, it's all I can think about." His eyes darkened as he stepped closer to me. I pressed my back against the glass that surrounded the balcony. "You. Your hypnotic eyes, smooth skin, the taste of your lips, your flesh, your nectar. I can't get enough of you."

"Horacio," his name came out on a shallow breath.

"Yes, Sierra?" His tongue moved across his bottom lip.

"You're dangerously close." I couldn't take my eyes off his lips as he moved even closer to me.

"I am." His hand was on my waist now, sliding up to cup my left "This isn't safe. We could get caught." I shuddered as he found my nipple, perky beneath the thin fabric of my dress.

"We could." He was so close to me that his breath brushed across my lips when he spoke.

"There would be repercussions for this." I swear I didn't tell my hands to travel around his waist and up the length of his back. Nor did I instruct my pelvis to thrust forward, giving him an unspoken invitation to continue his risky activity.

"Indeed, there would be."

"You don't seem to care." If I was honest, neither did I, but two people not caring about losing everything was a dangerous combination.

"Ms. Grey, at this moment in time, I cannot find it inside myself to give one fuck about the repercussions." His statement ended with a soft growl before his lips overtook my own. He kissed me with a hunger that felt like I could never satisfy, but dammit if I wouldn't enjoy trying.

He wasted not one more moment. His hand found the split in the side of my dress and ripped away the thong I wore beneath. Thank god it wasn't one of my favorites. Before I could react, he'd already released himself, pulled my leg up around his waist and slid inside of me. He lifted me just enough to perch my ass on the railing that wrapped around the balcony.

I bit down on his shoulder to muffle the moans. Odds were that no one would hear me over the music playing a level below us, but I didn't want to risk it. I neared my climax and right on cue he stopped, turned me around and entered me again, grabbing handfuls of my ass to guide each stroke.

The sound of the door opening and the smell of the food wafting out didn't register with my sense soon enough for us to avoid exposure. The glass shattered to the floor as I turned to see my friend and her future husband, who'd snuck away from the party to enjoy the view of the night sky, getting a full show of a different moon.

"Fuck." For half a second I considered continuing. Hell, we were already facing punishment. Might as well get an orgasm out of it.

CHAPTER
NINE

"You still think those bitches are your friends?" My sister couldn't wait long enough for the door to close behind her before she started her bitching. "I can't believe she turned you in."

"Camille how kind of you to visit." I'd been expecting her since I was taken from the Dark, my magic bound, and tossed in the holding cell.

Tana had, as Camille put it, turned me in. I told myself it was because her future husband was there. She was one of my closest friends. She loved me and wouldn't do this unless they forced her hand. Yeah, I told myself that even though I had a nagging feeling deep inside of my gut that told me she would have called the authorities, regardless. She was a Light, and at the end of the day, friend or no friend, they always did what they felt was right. Allowing me to fuck one of their most eligible men was not the proper thing to do.

"I told you to keep the pussy power on lockdown." Camille sat in the chair across from mine. "Now look at you, they've blocked your magic and locked you away."

"Why are you here?"

"I thought you'd want to know that your partner in crime is

also in lock up. Though with him being a man of the Light and from what I hear, a hot commodity in the procreation department, he'll get out long before you do."

"Do you come with any information pertinent to my status?" It was hard enough trying not to think about Horacio as it was. My focus had to be on my shit.

"Well, you've never had an issue before. Odds are you'll get a slap on the wrist for it. They'll also revoke your access to the Light."

"Revoke my access?" The knot in my stomach tightened as I processed what that meant. I would never see him again.

"Yeah, well they can't allow for you to go over there dirtying up the good men with your dark pussy."

"Could you please stop using that word?"

"Pussy? Why? It's such a grand word." She winked and blew a kiss to the guard who watched us through the window of the door.

"Sometimes I wish you'd never gone to that forsaken planet." Taking Camille to Earth had introduced her to new and disgusting ways to be Dark. Since we began our excursions, she'd picked up all the stereotypical bad girl traits she could find.

"I bet you're wishing that you never did either. Then your pussy wouldn't have gotten you into this shit."

"Go away."

"Why would you want me to go away?"

"Because I have more important things to worry about right now."

"Like this hideous attire?" She pointed at the bland gray pants and shirt that covered my body like an oversized pillow case. "It's not very flattering."

"Yeah, that's my biggest worry. Poor wardrobe options."

"Look, shit aside, I hope that this turns out okay for you." In an uncharacteristic move, Camille pulled me into a hug. "I don't want my sister to go to the Haze."

The door opened and the stoic guard stepped in. "No touching, you know the rule."

"Yeah, yeah, I know." She stepped back and fixed her fro. "Time for me to leave, anyway. I don't want the drab to rub off on me. Take care, sister."

Shortly after she'd left, the guard reappeared to take me back to my holding cell. As we walked through the dark halls, which were warded to prevent any unauthorized Conjurns from getting inside or any prisoners from getting out, I thought about how I ended up in that situation.

I thought about him and everything that had taken place in such a brief window of time. I couldn't have put my entire future on the line for sex. Albeit it was amazing sex, mind blowing, but it was still just sex. I'd avoided men for the very reason of not having my life derailed just for a good time, and here I was, bound and headed to await sentencing.

I refused to believe that I'd given up everything for a fun time. And like that, it hit me. Waves of feeling that I hadn't before been open to. Without my magic to shield me from the onslaught, it was there. A strange feeling battered me. My stomach turned and my heart raced. I looked at the guard, afraid that he could tell what I was experiencing.

By the time they locked me back in the sealed room, I was amid a full-on panic attack. His name blasted on a loop inside of my mind. Questions concerning his safety and wellbeing. My heart ached, twisted inside my chest when I considered that I may never see him again.

"What the fuck is this?" I muttered aloud and gripped the sides of the thin mattress on the cot they'd provided for me to enjoy my fitful nights on.

"Sierra?" His voice was there where it shouldn't be. Was this a side effect of this unnamed emotion that had my chest burning like it had set me on fire?

"Horacio?" I responded aloud as if he would materialize in front of me, though I knew it was impossible.

"Are you okay?" his voice faded in and out with the faulty connection

"Yes, are you?" I caught the guard walking by my holding cell and switched to speaking inside my mind. "Also, how am I hearing you in my head?"

"I don't know, but I'm glad it's there. Now, get out of there."

"What?" I kept my eye on the door. How long would it be before they realized what was going on?

"You're not safe."

"What are you talking about?"

"I've heard things here, things I'm sure I'm not supposed to hear, but they were talking about you. About the one with the odd eyes. Something about that seed we picked up."

"I'll be out of here soon, my sister just told me. I'll be home and I can figure this out."

"No, you don't understand. They don't plan on letting you out of there, Sierra."

"What?"

"Get out, now." He stopped talking and his voiced popped back into my head again. "Sierra, whatever you do, find a way to escape!"

"Horacio? Horacio? Fuck!" I've never understood how silence could be so suffocating until that moment, until I felt the connection snap in my head. It swallowed me whole and my breathing felt hallow. I stood and pressed my back against the wall. My hair was pinned up to keep it out of my face, but it felt too tight. Releasing the wrap, I felt it, a small gift from my sister tucked away in the coils of my hair. Removing the object from my hair, I recognized what it was.

A symbol I'd seen and practiced countless times as a child was sketched on the surface of the small tablet. This was my way out. I stared at it, considering what would happen if I ingested it. I'd be free, but at a cost. The burning started again in my chest along with a new sensation, a stabbing pain in my gut. Horacio.

I popped the tablet in my mouth and the fizzy sensation that started on my tongue spread throughout my body. I looked down at my hand as it faded away. Guess I'm going to see mom.

CHAPTER
TEN

"Sierra, so good of you to visit." It was the same tone my sister had. She inherited the nerve grating sound from the one who birthed us. The tablet had stolen me from my cell and dropped me right into my mother's study.

"Mother." The tingles were still working their way through my body as I finished materializing. Being transported created a disruptive sensation. The process ripped apart your body into a trillion little pieces, transported through the air, and then put back together on the other side. It was a good thing my mother was a pro at this magic form. I'd seen it done wrong which resulted in a shattered soul.

"I wish it were under better circumstances, but I'm sure you're aware that I'd been trying to get your sister to get you here for quite some time." My mother was a full-figured vixen who looked so much like me that most people mistook us for twins.

It was her body, her wide hips, plump ass, and full chest that bombarded me in my mid-twenties and garnered the unwanted attention from the opposite sex. Yet another reason for the tension between us. My relationship had always been rocky with my mother. I was the youngest of two girls, both by different fathers who we would grow up never knowing. I despised her for that, but as an adult I realized that it wasn't her fault. Those were the cards dealt to the wicked ones. We didn't get the forever love. In the Dark, if a relationship happened at all, it was short lived. Couples didn't pair up and make life long promises to procreate and build together.

It was what my sister teased me about. I wanted something that was unheard of for our kind. I questioned time and time again why that was the case. Even if we were Dark, why did that mean we were incapable of love? That was my theory, which every adult I'd encountered dismantled. Love implied that you were open to Light. It couldn't thrive in a cold dark environment and being a Dark Conjurn meant that no light could ever touch your heart or soul. Whenever I would refute this to my mother, she dished out the worst punishments she could conjure up. She wanted me to fall in line and be a good little girl like my sister.

When I exited Mastery and came back to the Dark. She was waiting for me, smug in herself righteousness. My family knew I felt I belonged in the Light. My heart could feel. I felt things that no Dark had ever experienced and yet there I was, ashened and marked for the Dark. She couldn't contain herself. Her gloating was too much to deal with. The job at the Hull was a means to get away from my mother. I worked hard and earned enough power to cut myself off from her. It had been a decade since I walked away from her.

"My address hasn't changed. If you had something to say you could have come yourself."

"Guys, could we not do this right now?" Camille entered the study. "If they haven't figured out that she's gone yet, it won't be long before they do. I'm already implicated in this, so we better make the best of this time."

"Your sister is right. There are much bigger things to worry about. Like your coming demise."

"Demise?"

"Well, yes. That's what I've been trying to warn you of, Sierra. The prophecy of your birth has come to fruition."

"What prophecy? What the hell are you talking about?" I looked to Camille because I trusted her over my mother, and she wore the look of a dog who'd chewed his master's shoes and gotten caught with the leather still hanging from his jaw. "There was no prophecy of my birth remember, that was the great disappointment for you. My eyes meant nothing."

"Your eyes meant everything, Sierra." She waved me off, already exhausted by our conversation. "I just never told you or anyone else. I hoped like hell you'd be like the red-tailed girl and that none of this would come true. Yet here we are, and here you are doing what they foretold."

"And what's that?"

"Messing with the balance of things." She frowned as she turned her dark eyes on me. "Fraternizing with the Light."

"I don't have time for this."

"Sister, please wait." Camille grabbed my hand, knowing that I was about to make a break for it. "Just listen to what she has to say."

"Okay, fine, I'm listening."

"Good." Our mother waved her hand over a small tray and a bowl of boiling water appeared. She pulled a small pouch from her pocket and emptied the contents in the bowl. The steam rose from the bowl and illustrated her story, beginning with a younger version of herself with a protruding belly. "When I was pregnant with you, I saw. It was a message sent to me by the ancients. They sent a young girl to me with eyes like yours and she told me you would be born different. She said that you would hold within yourself the capacity to change life as we knew it. Your birth was the sign of a coming change and of turmoil for all Conjurns."

"Change and turmoil," I repeated the words and understood my mother's fear. Conjurns hated change and would see it as nothing but a threat. That prophecy would have inspired fear. Enough fear that they would have separated me from my mother as soon as I was born. It didn't happen often, but it happened.

"If you go on with this man from the Light, it will lead to catastrophic events." She held my gaze with her sorrow filled eyes. "I know it in my heart. We haven't had the best relationship, and that is my fault. I was trying to protect you, but I should have been preparing you for this day."

"What does that mean? What is going to happen?"

"I cannot say."

"Once again, you're going to hide this shit from me? You're telling me that my life and the lives of everyone around me are on the line, but you won't tell me what the hell I'm up against."

"You know how this works. I can't tell you. It will only cause you to fulfill the prophecy if I do."

"I'm so done with—," a burning feeling that started from my stomach and shot up my throat. I clutched my hands around my neck and fell to the floor in agony.

"What's happening?" Camille dropped to my side and looked up at our mother. "Why is she hurting?"

"They must know." My mother looked down on me and cried. "They are trying to sever the bond."

"The bond? What bond?"

"The one between you and the man of the Light. You two were destined to meet, destined to mate, and destined to end life as we know it for Dynundria."

"You have got to be shitting me." Camille held my face between her hand. "Sierra, breathe. You're going to be okay."

I heard it then as I felt it. His pain. He screamed out, and the sound filled my mind. "I have to go," I said through tears. "They're hurting him. I can feel it."

"Sierra, you can't." Camille helped me to my feet. "They are holding him in the Light. You can't go there. They have shut the passageway off to you and even if you could, how do you expect to get away? They will kill you."

"So, you expect me to sit here, knowing what they are doing to him and do nothing?"

"If you go there, we lose you," my mother spoke. "That's it. There is no going back here and you can't stay there. The only other place for you is—"

"The Haze," Camille finished her thought. "Do you want to give up everything and end up there?"

"Look. I can't explain it. I don't understand what's happening. Maybe had our mother been more forthcoming with me, I would know what to tell you right now. What I know is that there is a searing pain inside of me and I know that's only a drop in the bucket compared to what they are putting him through. What I feel is unknown to me. It's intense and overwhelming. It blocks out all forms of logic or desire for simple self-preservation. I cannot and will not let him suffer alone."

"It's love."

"What?"

"No Dark should feel it but you baby girl, you are different. They foretold it. You possess something that none of us do." She grabbed my hands in hers. "You love that man and you must do what you feel is right."

"Mother!"

"Camille, she has to do this. I wish it weren't true. I wish that I could protect her. It's all I've ever tried to do, but this is her destiny. She is fated to follow this path and we cannot stop her."

"Sierra—"

"Camille. I love you. You're a total pain in my ass most days, but I love you." I pulled her into a hug. "Please take care of Maleficent for me. And remember to always feed her before you take a bath."

"What?" Camille sniffled.

"The girl has issues." I smiled.

"That cat hates me, but I promise I will take care of her," she laughed. "Wait, how are you going to get to him?"

"I did it once before. I don't know how, but I moved across the border with no passageway. If I could figure that out..."

"You teleported," my mother announced. "It happens when couples are truly connected on a hire plane. You can move yourself through space to be with that person. It's the basics of the tablets I make. I tie a bit of my essence into each one, which then allows whoever consumes it, to find me. There is a rare bond that exists between you. I don't know how, but it's there."

"The seed."

"What?"

"The Origin Seed. Our mission was to retrieve it while we were on Earth." I looked at the palm of my hand. "I touched it and then we—"

"I knew it!"

"Oh, shut up."

"That's it. There is a connection between you two, the contact with the seed must have strengthened that."

"So, how do I make this work?"

"In theory, you just have to focus on being with him. Think of nothing but him. The touch of his skin, the sound of his voice, everything about him."

I did as instructed and as my mind filled with thoughts of Horacio, my body faded from the room.

"Please be careful," Sierra spoke.

When I opened my eyes again, I could see nothing but blood.

CHAPTER
ELEVEN

"Horacio!" I fell to my knees next to his blood covered body. So much for the Light being better than the Dark. Fresh lacerations covered his body. The monsters left his face swollen and bloodied.

"Sierra, what are you doing here? How did you get here?" He coughed as I cradled his head in my lap.

"Did you expect me to stand by and let them continue to hurt you? I felt it. Everything they did to you." The tears fell from my eyes.

"I'm fine," he coughed and spit up blood. "I'll be fine. You shouldn't be here. If they catch you here, I don't know what they'll do to you."

"What the hell did they do to you?"

"What I deserve. Maybe less; I broke the rules. This was my punishment."

"What happened to the Light being so much better than the Dark? I thought your people were flush with compassion and empathy for others. This happens for you after one transgression?"

"I'll be okay." His words didn't match the feeling in my gut that told me if I didn't get him away from there, I would lose him forever. He wouldn't make it out of that holding cell.

"We're getting out of here."

"And going where? They will come after us."

"I don't care. Look, I can't go home. I risked everything to come here for you. There is no way in hell I'm going to leave you here to deal with this on your own."

"Shh, they're coming," he hushed me as a group of guards walked past the holding cell. They didn't look in on the one they'd left in a pool of his own blood. None of them cared about his survival after he'd mixed with a Dark. As their foot falls faded away he spoke. "How do you suggest we get out of here?"

"Our bond brought me here. It's what I used that night when I was in your bed. It wasn't a dream like I thought, I was there with you. Maybe we can use that same energy to get us out of here."

"What do we do?"

"Just focus your mind on a safe space. Reach out to it." I grabbed his hands in my own. "Let your heart take you there and mine will follow you."

"My magic doesn't work here."

"Your magic is, but ours isn't. There is something different about us now, I can't explain it." I kissed his lips and breathed some of my energy into him. In normal circumstances, transferring my dark energy to him wouldn't work. These weren't normal circumstance. It didn't matter that I was Dark, and he was Light. The connection between Horacio and I was something unheard of. "Trust me, please."

Horacio did as I asked. He relaxed and let his heart and mind find a place where he could find safety from the horrors inside the cell. As he did, his body faded, and I could feel my heart, the fresh energy that flowed through me, reaching out to follow. He hadn't completed the transition before the guards returned. I prayed that they would walk by again without notice, but this time, one guard checked on the man they'd left for dead. He sounded the alarm as Horacio faded from my arms.

The door burst open, and I stood there, drab gray clothing covered in the blood of my lover and pissed. Without hesitation, they launched their attack.

"Get her!" the man furthers from me shouted as three others entered the cell and surrounded me. There were four guards in total. Four men who would rather die than let me out of that room.

"Where is the man?" They scanned the room, looking under the bunk and in the small nook where he would store his clothing.

"He isn't here."

"What did you do to him?" the head guard, marked by the three striped on his left shoulder, asked me.

"He is safe from you."

"You're a dumb bitch for coming here. Do you think you're going to make it out of this room alive?"

"Oh, I'll be just fine." I smiled because I had a secret they were unaware of. "It's you who have to worry."

Their leader nodded, giving the signal for the others to restrain me. Two guards grabbed my arms while the other attempted to blind me by putting a hood over my face. I could have left. It would take nothing to focus my energy and go to Horacio wherever he was. It was my anger that stopped me from doing that. Anger inspired by what they'd done to Horacio. And by what my people would no doubt do to me if I ever returned home. It made me furious that it was such a fucking crime for me to care about another person. It pissed me off that my mother hid this secret from me. I had so much anger inside of me and four men to take it out on.

It was a unique thing, being able to tap into my power without limitation. I could feel the wards of the building trying to contain me, but it was easy to break free. Each guard wore a special medallion tucked under their shirts that would allow their magic to work at a lower rate. This was to avoid abuse of power. In theory, I should have been defenseless to them.

I shifted my weight, dropping low beneath the hood, and slipped from the hold they had on my arms. When they regained their footing, they reached for me again. This time I was ready for them. I loved playing with fire and this was the perfect time. Blue flames rose from the ground, creating a circle around me that stretched out. The flames swallowed the two closest to me and they fell to the floor screaming as their flesh melted. The third, who tried to place the hood on my head, ran for the exit. Another one of my favorites, telekinesis. I was told this was a skill I got from my father.

He almost reached the door before my mind grabbed him, pulling him back to me. I could taste the fear from him. I could feel his struggle; he wanted to live. He pleaded with his leader to help save him. But they gave him no aid as the coward ran, leaving him behind to suffer alone. I almost felt sorry for him. Almost. The thud of his body echoed, the sound of his neck snapping as he slammed against the floor. The others were still groaning from the pain of the fire as I faded from the room. "They'll come here first you know." I stood in Horacio's bedroom. He'd already regained his strength. Without the restriction on his magic, he could heal himself. He stood with a towel, cleaning the blood from his face.

"Yes, but I had to come here. There are things here we will need." He headed for the closet and emerged with a pre-packed duffle bag.

"You knew this would happen." I eyed the bag he slung over his shoulder.

"A prophet told my father. He kept it from me until he was on his death bed. Even then he was too afraid to tell me. Instead he left me this scavenger hunt of clues that explained about you and the prophecy foretold of our coming together. Still, I have so many questions. I tried my best to research and find an answer. When the call to work with the Dark came, I had to take it. I had to know if you were real. My father had a thing for pulling pranks. That night heading home, I'd given up. I was ready to hang it all up and go back to my normal life, maybe find a good Light girl to be with. But then I saw you. The girl with those spectacular eyes."

"So, both our parents hid this from us. Great. Now we get the fun of trying to figure this out on our own. And we get to do that while outrunning the hunters. No doubt the powers that be have already dispatched them to find us."

"I have a plan, if you trust me."

What choice did I have? I had no plan at all, and the Dark and Light was going to be coming down on us. "What's your plan? Let me guess, you want to follow the rules. Go back and take our punishments, then stay away from each other."

"No."

"No?"

"I don't care if hell rains down on Dynundria. The time that I've spent with you is the most alive I've ever felt. I'm not giving that up."

"How do you feel? I feel strange." I sat on the bed. "Ever since I touched that damn seed. It's like something else is taking over me. Something else is controlling me making my desires override my brain." I thought of the men I'd left on the floor of his holding cell. I'd done nothing like that before, but I'd be lying if I said it didn't feel amazing.

"Is that a good thing?" He pulled a fresh shirt over his head and joined me on the bed.

"I'm not sure. I've always played it safe. It would be easy to place the blame on you, but I'm the wicked girl who has always played by the rules. Fear kept me from doing anything viewed as reckless or troubling. There is a tightrope for anyone of the Dark who wants even a bit the privilege given to the Light. All I wanted was to keep my friends. Friends who have turned their backs on me now. How boring."

"I know the feeling. I've always done the right thing, followed the rules. Hell, even now I was willing to accept whatever they dished out to me. I told myself I deserved it."

"What's our next move?"

"It's obvious that this goes to the top of the chain. From what I heard inside that cell; they've been expecting this. I'm sure the only reason they allowed me to go on the mission was because I have no marker. They couldn't be sure who you were meant to be with." He pulled my hand into his. "There aren't many people that we can trust. There is only one place we can go where we can regroup."

"The Haze." I knew where he was going with his thinking.

It was the only place that made sense. It could also be the place to make us the most vulnerable. Entering the Haze would mean giving up our abilities.

"Yes. I know the risk, but it's the best option available to us now. It's too bad the pods aren't ready for another launch. We could go back to Earth."

"People who go there don't come back." I looked him in the eyes. "If we go to the Haze, we give up everything."

"We've already given up everything. What benefits us is that the people who live there don't know who we are. Odds are no one has reached out to tell them about us either."

"Are you sure?"

"No, but what other choice do we have now?"

"Right, when do we leave?"

The explosion shook the building. My ears rang as I clutched the man at my side and found his face to make sure he was okay. He nodded at me, affirming that he had not been further injured. I grabbed hold of Horacio and looked up to see the ball of fire hurling through the sky aimed for his bedroom. My hand lifted to a point just in time for it to slam into the window, sending glass shards flying in on us.

JESSICA CAGE

CHAPTER

TWELVE

I clutched my chest and gasped for air as my feet landed on the tan dirt. We'd only just made it out of his home before the second assault. Horacio had the place shielded; he'd been ready for every probable outcome, including the need for a one use portal to carry us to the Haze. The device was a product of science with a touch of magic and set to self-destruct after one use.

"Sorry about that," he coughed, clearing his own lungs. "I figure this was the best way. Without using our magic, we didn't leave a signature to trace. By the time they find someone who can figure out the mechanism we used. We should have been able to prepare ourselves for their arrival."

"That's if they haven't figured out where we've gone without needing that device. They won't find us in the Light or the Dark, there's only one other place to look."

"That should still give us a few days to prepare. They will think coming here neutralized our magic."

"How did you know that thing would work?"

"I've tested it, granted not on such long distances and not in the Haze, but I have tested it. My tests proved that it could make it across the borders undetected, which is why I used science to engineer it."

"How is it you're so smart?"

"My father, he demanded it. I often thought it was unfair, my brothers are average, my sister is a brat who couldn't tell her left hand from her right, but he always expected so much more from me. Now I understand why."

"He knew what you'd be facing."

"I'm guessing your mother was just as hard on you?"

"Hell, she is the reason I am who I am now. Strong, determined to prove the world wrong."

"Tough love."

"Yeah, right?" I looked out into the gray distance that provided no clarity of our location. It was impossible to measure our distance from the principal city, but our current area was pretty much deserted. The horizon was a flat gray line. "Guess we walk now."

He reached into his bag and pulled out a small gray box, which he sat on the ground in front of us. "Walking won't be necessary."

"I hate to tell you this, but I don't think your little box can support the two of us."

"Well, not in that form." He laughed, reached down and pressed the sides of the box in. There was a snapping sound followed by a pop of smoke and when it cleared, a solar car sat in front of us.

"How is that possible?"

"Well, I stored magic inside of these devices. This way it's not neutralized when coming into the Haze. There is a hitch, however. There is a one use limit for each box."

"You're a genius."

"I'm only a genius if you don't get burned in the process," he joked and pointed to my feet, reminding me of the speedy shoes he'd created before.

"Well, let's hope sitting in this thing doesn't burn my ass off." I climbed into the passenger side with his help.

As we drove, I expected to see buildings coming into view. I expected to witness life in the Haze. There should have been millions of people in the Haze. I was excited to experience what it was all like. In Mastery we were only given a brief description. To be in the Haze was to no longer have access to the outside world, and it was also to have privacy from that which you walked away from.

Instead of taking in the beautiful new scenery and finding the faces of people to welcome us, we were met with a horrid stench. As we neared the city, it washed over us and was so bad I thought I would vomit right there in the car. There were no people, sounds, or signs of life.

"What the hell is this?" I peered out of the window and covered my nose.

"Something isn't right." Horacio slowed the car down to a crawl.

"Where is everyone? What the hell is that stench?"

"Death," he said in a morbid tone.

"Excuse me?"

"I've smelled it before, it would linger after one of my father's failed experiments. He was a doctor and often practiced new treatments on expired Conjurns because their body still kept traces of their magic. This odor, I've never experienced it so potent, but it is the same."

81

"Horacio," I looked back at him, turning my eyes from the empty streets. "There is no one here. They're all dead."

"That can't be true."

"Look around, there is no life here. Where are the people? So many chose life in the Haze, it should be just as full of life as the Light or the Dark and yet there is nothing here."

"There has to be someone here. We will keep looking."

We drove for two hours. Two hours of empty streets and the stench that got worse as we went on. About an hour in, we saw evidence of life, or lack thereof. Decaying bodies were laid out in the streets. People who had dropped right where they stood. My heart broke as we passed the bodies of a mother and her two small children. They would have been on their way to Mastery soon, to make a choice for their lives. I held back the tears as we drove on.

"There, up ahead." Horacio pointed to a flickering light in the distance. "Do you see that?"

"Yes, is that fire?"

"If there is fire that means someone is still alive here."

"Let's hope so."

The car stopped in front of a building that looked like it would topple over at any moment. One good gust of wind and it would cave in. We exited the car and though there was evidence that there was no life around us, we watched our surroundings as we climbed the steps. I was careful not to disturb any of the bodies we passed. The door to the building was unlocked. We entered and were met with an herbal scent that, though it was pungent, was a welcomed relief from the smell of decaying flesh.

Though the inside had a better fragrance, it wasn't in better shape. The floors were covered in trash and animal excrement, the walls looked as if someone had started demolition on the interior. The first sign of life we saw was a Skenadira. It was a mutation of a wolf spider which was brought from Earth and for a time was a major problem in Dynundria. We were careful to avoid its webs as we climbed the stairs to the second floor. To touch one would cause instant paralysis, allowing for an easy target for the oversized creature.

"The light was up here; we should be able to find it. Keep your eyes open," Horacio said as he took the lead, heading down the hall to the left of the landing.

We took our time as we moved down the hall and once again were careful not to disturb anything around us. The building's structure was sketchy, and Horacio had valid concerns about whether it would support the activity now happening within its walls. The floors creaked beneath our footsteps as we continued on, warning us of its fragility.

I held my breath as we proceeded. The building was filled with the echoes of the life that was once there. Sounds that I knew I shouldn't be hearing rang out around me. It was the cries of children who'd lost their mothers, the friends who grieved over the companions,. The overwhelming emotions of a million people slammed into me and with every footstep that brought me closer to that room, those emotions became stronger. Before long, they were so overpowering that I couldn't move any further.

Horacio looked back to find me hunched over, trying to find a way to push through. "Sierra, are you okay? What happened?"

I lifted my head but struggled to see him through the tears that had flooded my eyes and blurred my vision. These tears were not my own, this pain belonged to someone else. The heart ache I that burned the center of my chest was not mine to claim.

When I didn't respond, he grabbed my face between the palm of his hands. "Are you okay? Do you need to turn back?"

"No, we can't," I struggled to speak. "We have to keep going."

"Not if it's hurting you like this."

"No, we keep going because it's hurting. I feel it," I sobbed. "It's all of their pain. We have to figure out what the hell happened here."

"Are you sure? We can stop, so you can rest."

"Horacio, do I look like a child? I'll be fine. Besides, we don't have the luxury of time to wait around for me to feel better. Let's just get this done." I forced my body to stand upright, even though every fiber of my being was now coated in several layers of other people's agony.

He nodded, understanding my commitment to the task, and resumed his route. We made it to the door, but before opening it, he rested his hand on the frame. His eyes closed as he tried to get a feel for what waited on the other side. A moment later he looked back at me with unsure eyes. I tilted my head forward. I got it, there was the danger of the unknown.

The door opened with a low creak as he turned the knob and pushed it. We found the source of the herbal smell that filled the place. The rush of air smacked us in the face with its potency. On the other side of the door was an empty room. In the middle of the floor sat a small woman surround it by a barrier of ever-burning herbs. As one turned to ash, another emerged to take its place. It was an intricate spell that could take months to perform. It was no accident that we found her.

Her eyes were open, looking down at her folded lap, which cradled a book held in her clutches. We couldn't hear her words but her lips moved as if she was reading from the book, but when I glanced at the pages, they were blank.

"What are we supposed to do now?" he looked at me as if I had an answer for his question.

"I don't know." I kneeled in front of her. "The real question is if she is even still in there. With the barrier placed around her, there could be so many things going on in there. She may be a shell, hell she could be the reason for all of this. If she is in there and this is just some sort of self-inflicted trance, well. you know the basics of spell casting. If we break the trance and interrupt whatever she's doing now, it's going to cause untold consequences for both her and everyone around her."

"What people?" he chuckled, finding humor where I saw none. He wasn't inflicted with the pain of the Haze like I was. "We're the only ones here."

"We don't know that for sure. And even if we were the only people here, I would prefer not to cause some unknown catastrophe while I'm standing two feet away from the source."

"So, what do you suggest we do then?"

"We have to reach her on the other side wherever she is. Right now she isn't with us." I looked around for anything that we could use but came up short until I noticed the bag strapped to his back. "Got anything in that magical bag that could help us out here? Without our magic to help us, we're screwed."

"I think I may have something." He pulled the bag from his back and started digging through the contents. "I should have thought of this before!" A minute later he pulled out another one of the small gray boxes and set it on the floor in front of the entranced woman.

"What is it supposed to be?" I stood and took a step back from the box, just in case it transformed into a makeshift lab.

"Well, if I did it right, it's an awakening spell." He smiled, proud of himself for having forgotten about having the one thing we could use in this moment.

"Not that I'm not thrilled, but why would you have an awakening spell?"

"Because of my father's notes. It was one clue he left for me to find. I didn't question it, I just made it happen," he shrugged as he adjusted the shell of the box to engage the spell. "Figured better safe than sorry."

"Well, at least your father did more than my mother to prepare us for this situation."

"Alright, stand back." He grabbed held his arm out, ushering me back towards the door as the box emitted a cool blue smoke that surrounded the woman.

Before the smoke cleared, we heard one thing whispered through the air, "Sierra Grey."

CHAPTER
THIRTEEN

"Did she just say my name?" I peered through the smoke at the woman who now had her eyes locked on me.

"Yes, she did."

"Why?" I asked him and he shrugged, so I turned my questioning to the woman. "How do you know me? What do you want?"

"The child will be born with mis colored eyes." she spoke in an eerie monotone. "She will be the one to avenge those who were wronged."

"What?"

"Wait," Horacio grabbed my shoulder and nodded towards the book in her lap. As she spoke, the pages filled with her words.

"An imbalance will come. Conjurns will become extinct, unless she so saves them all. Devour the seed, give life for life. She must restore the balance." Her eyes closed and her head fell forward.

"Okay, what the hell was that?" I snapped at Horacio.

"I'm not sure." He moved towards the woman but jumped back we she gasped and fell forward. He took several deep breaths before looking up to me.

"Do you know who I am?"

She nodded.

"Do you know why I am here?"

She nodded again.

"Please tell me what I am supposed to do."

She lifted her finger to her forehead, pressed it against her lips and then touched the pages of the book, filling them with text. When the words stopped forming, she fell forward. Dead.

I couldn't move. I just looked at her hunched over the book, lifeless. Horacio reached out to remove the book from her grip and when he did, she crumbled.

"She kept all of this in her mind, that's what she was doing." He flipped through the pages. "She had to protect this knowledge. For you."

"For me? She did this to herself for me?"

"Look," he handed me the book. "Everything you've been questioning, it's all there."

We found a room where we could sit and read the contents of the pages. Everything was there, the prophecy of my birth and the man who I would love. The fall of the Haze and eventually all Conjurns. Our numbers were dwindling, and it wasn't because the women were choosing to have fewer babies. Our people were becoming sterile.

The Leaders of the Light and Dark did a horrible thing to keep our numbers. During something they called the Glorious Return, they stole the life force from every Conjurn in the Haze and fed it into their own territories. It wasn't enough. All they did was create a temporary fix. The prophecy calls for a greater sacrifice. One life, one extraordinary life to be sacrificed to restore balance and prevent the fall of Dynundria. If the Conjurns died out, the planet would suffer. Our lives were irrevocably tied to it. Every species outside of our own would become extinct.

"I'm supposed to kill myself." I looked at him.

"There has to be another way."

"It says it clear as day. I'm supposed to swallow the Origin Seed. If I don't all of Dynundria will fall. Not just our people, everything on this planet will die." I closed the book and stared at the worn leather cover. "I have to do this. I can't be that selfish. I can't save myself and let so many others die."

"Sierra—"

"Horacio," I stopped him. "Meeting you was the best thing that has ever happened to me because it made me realize that I am not broken. I'm who I'm supposed to be. A Dark Conjurn who can feel. I thought maybe it meant that I was supposed to come to a realization that the Mastery was wrong and that I belonged with you. That wasn't it, though. I had to be able to feel everything that happened here. Their pain, their sorrow. How else could they have expected me to make this decision?"

"I refuse to lose you."

"Looks like you won't have much of a choice in the matter." I stood from the table and headed for the exit.

"Where are you going?"

"Where I belong; home."

"Do you have a plan? How will you get back?" He followed me out of the building to where the car waited.

"Figured, we could drive back to the border." I pointed to the bag he carried. "I'm sure you created something to help us get back. Your father would have known this would happen."

"Yes, but—"

"But nothing. This is the way it is."

"The sun is going down. We won't be able to make it back."

"Looks like we have one more night together."

It took us an hour to find a stable building to lie in. Inside of his bag was an odor neutralizer, handy as ever, that we used to seal the small home off from the smell that had me ready to vomit. The showers still worked. We took advantage of the opportunity to clean ourselves up. Ever prepared, he packed the trunk of the car with food, clean drinking water, and fresh clothing.

"I can't believe you're forcing me to give this up." He kissed my forehead. We lay in the bed together, watching the stars outside the window. My head rested on his chest as he held me in his arms.

"Give what up?"

"You," he chuckled. "As if it weren't obvious. I don't want to let go of this moment and any chance of moments like it in the future."

"You'll live and find someone new to love and grow with. You'll have more moments." My voice betrayed me and cracked with my emotions.

"Sierra."

"Yes?" I looked up at him.

"Don't do this."

"How many times are you going to ask me that?"

"Until you say yes, or until I can't ask it anymore."

"Okay, let's not be so somber now." I lifted myself up, threw my leg over him so I was sitting on top of him, and kissed him. "There will be plenty of time for tears later. This may be my last night alive. I want to enjoy myself."

"As you wish."

We spent the next twelve hours wrapped in each other. Horacio worked my body bringing me to climax time and time again as he attempted to put a lifetime of loving on me in one night. When the sun rose on the Haze, the fire began.

FOURTEEN

"Do you see that?" I squinted as I viewed the distance outside of the window. There was a gray cloud slowly approaching the house we'd claimed for ourselves for the night. "What is that?"

"It looks like smoke," Horacio answered as he pulled his shirt over his head.

"Smoke," I turned to him. "Smoke from what?"

"Fire," he pointed just as the flamed came into view. The glow reached up into the center of the cloud giving it a terrifying glow. "We have to go. Now!"

We it made to the car just as the cloud of smoke reached us and right behind it was the blaze. It engulfed everything in its path creating a thunderous sound as buildings collapsed and engines of abandoned vehicles exploded from the heat. The tires skidded against the ground pushing the car forward before I could fully shut my door. We hadn't made it to the next block of homes before the house was taken over by the smoke.

"We have to hurry. If it overtakes us, it could block out the sun." I looked through the rear window at the approaching threat. "How long do you think we can drive without direct sunlight?"

"I don't know, but not long. I didn't think of making this thing to code. A typical solar energy stores a few days' worth of energy, this will give us a matter of hours at best but it's not fully charged now. The sun hasn't been up long enough."

"Well I suggest you get this thing moving faster."

"I'm going as fast as I can but we can't outrun it. Our best chance is to try to find a way to stop it from further progressing." He started shifting his weight in his seat. "You have to take the wheel."

"Why?" I grabbed the wheel as he released it. "What are you going to do?"

"I need to look in the bag." He fell into the back seat.

"The bag of tricks. Good!" I cheered not knowing if he had anything capable of stopping a fire cloud from chasing us.

In a clumsy effort I took over driving, only nearly hitting one building just before slamming through a pile of decaying bodies. I engaged the windshield wipers to remove the carnage from the window and whispered an apology to the deceased.

"This should work." He held another box in his hand, only this time it was blue in color.

"That one looks different from the others you've used."

"It's a defense cube. Something we can use to protect ourselves. This one contains a barrier wall. It's made similar to the magic used to reinforce the borders between territories. It wasn't designed for this, but it should hold back the smoke, at least until the pressure builds."

"Pressure?" I trained my eyes on the road determined not to harm another body even though the fire behind us would not take the same care.

"Eventually there will be too much pressure with the growing fire. It will break free. But it should buy us enough time to make it to the border wall."

"Sounds good enough to me. Do it."

He engaged the box and threw it out of the window. A few moments later, there was a flash of light that shot up into the sky and out to either side for miles. We both held the air in our lungs as the cloud of smoke met the new barrier. It stopped; the damned thing worked and we both regained the ability to breathe.

"We're good. We're going to make it." He settled in the seat next to me. "I can take over driving again."

"I'm okay to drive." I relaxed into the seat, checking the rearview mirror one more time.

"You're about to sacrifice yourself for the fate of the world. At least let me drive you to the event."

"I'm about to sacrifice myself for the fate of the world," I repeated his statement and glanced at him. "At least let me drive myself there."

"Understood." He nodded and grabbed my right hand from the wheel and laced his fingers with mine. "Is holding your hand while you drive okay?"

"Yes it is." I laughed. "Thank you."

The closer we got to the border, the worse the trapped cloud looked behind us. I feared we wouldn't actually make it, but we did. I pulled the car to a stop and we climbed out. Horacio looked at the cloud which stretched up into the sky.

"It won't be long until it breaks." He grabbed his bag from the back seat.

"So, we need to get out of here before it does. How do you suggest we do that? Another box?"

He turned to me with another gray box resting in the palm of his hand. "You know it."

"You know, I'm going to miss those boxes."

"We'll have no need for them when you get back home. Your power should return to you." He activated the box and placed it on the ground right next to the wall. As he stepped back the humming began. "You ready to go?"

"What exactly will this do?" I stepped back, following his lead.

"It's going to open a passageway; it will work like the others." He paused, "Only it won't remain open for quite as long. Eventually the magic of the border wall will degrade it."

"How long will is stay open?" I asked as the wall began to split.

"Not long, we have to move quickly." He held out his hand to me.

"We do this together." I smiled.

"Together." He nodded and we ran for it.

The wall slammed shut, sealing it once again from the Haze. I was relieved to find that we'd landed in the Dark, where my magic was its strongest. To test the theory I brought a small flame to the tip of my finger.

"Okay this is your territory." His lips lowered to my finger as he blew out the flame. "I think we've had enough fire for one day. What do we do now?"

"We go to my house." I straightened my clothing, the cross over left me looking like I'd been in a wrestling match.

"Do you think it will be safe there? I mean you did just escape prison not too long ago. How do you know they aren't on the lookout for you?"

"Oh, its fine. I would be able to feel it if the wards at my house had been broken. If anything, the reports of my being in the Light and breaking out the hunky guy, have them looking anywhere but my home." I held my hand out to him. "Come on, let's go."

We landed in the middle of my living room. I half expected my annoying sister to be there waiting for me, but she was not. Maleficent was though. She whined as she sauntered up to me. Already she was being poorly cared for. So much for my Camille taking her in. I headed for the kitchen as Horacio looked around. It felt weird having him there. I felt exposed as if that made any sense at all. The man had seen me from angles that I couldn't begin to describe and yet I was nervous about him finding out that I wasn't the tidiest Conjurn around.

In the kitchen I found my fat cat's bowl overrunning with food and on the counter with a note in my sisters handwriting, "I tried!" It would appear that Maleficent wasn't on board with our arrangement for her new ownership.

"I really wish you would have gone with her." I knelt down to rub behind her ears. "Who's going to take care of you now?"

Horacio walked in, catching my adoring moment and before I could acknowledge him, my hand was abandoned mid rub. Maleficent purred as she rubbed the side of her belly against his leg.

I chuckled at his worried expression, "Well, it looks like she belongs to you now."

"W-what?" he stuttered as heavy paws began to pet the side of his calf.

"Cats choose their owners. She chose me when I got back from Mastery. I asked my sister to care for her but it was a long shot. The two of them never got along. Come to mind, Malefi-cent never likes anyone, but it looks like that's changed."

"She's got good taste." He waggled his eyebrows and laughed.

"That she does." I took his arm and lifted the sleeve that hid his wrist.

"What are you doing?" he asked as I revealed mine.

"All this knowledge in your head and you know nothing of feline care? Did you skip that class in Mastery?" I held my wrist next to his. A thin string of light shone from beneath my flesh. It unraveled itself and moved to his before fading beneath his flesh. "Now she is yours. Wherever you go she will find you."

"Right, I guess I better read up on it then."

"Yeah, you better." I winked at him and then at the cat who looked far too pleased with herself. "Okay, I just need to grab a few things and then we can head out. No one's been here but it won't be long until they realize that I'm back."

CHAPTER
FIFTEEN

My arrival at the Hull was unexpected. They hadn't fortified the gates. Standard protocol called to have the perimeter reinforced. It should have happened the second I escaped. It was unlike Kianna to miss such an important detail. She was the face of the Hull, more than a secretary she ran the place. Whenever there was even a hint of a threat, she would have the barrier enhanced. The same sleepy guard sat in his stone tower. Again, I would have expected Kianna to ensure that a more reputable guard replaced him.

I'd never considered there would be a day when I would break into the place, but there I was, holding two activated red boxes in my hand, red for defense, as I caught the guard's eye. I threw the boxes towards the iron barrier that stood in my way and braced for impact. The first explosion weakened the gate and set off the alarms, the second sent it flying in broken pieces that littered the ground.

I sprinted forward and before I made it far beyond the broken gate; the guards exited the building in droves. For a moment I fear threatened to choke me. I was fearful that I would not make it. They had orders, their formation relayed what those orders were. With the weapons they brought to their hands, their goal was execution. And then something more powerful replaced my fear. Determination. I had to move forward. Determined to save my people, even if the idiots didn't understand, that's what I was doing.

I called to every fiber of magic inside me and received the pulsing of something else surge to the top. Wrapped in the emotions of all those who were lost to us, remnants of their power, power from the Haze. I held my hands out in front of me as I continued to run and let their power protect me.

Their footfalls thundered behind me. They had me surrounded, but I kept pushing forward. Their spirits moved to cut the offenders off from me. The barrier of magic that surrounded my body tightened as more Conjurn guards joined the surrounding ranks. Just as I thought they would break through; I saw the little red box drop from the sky. I knelt, crossed my arms above my head and tightened the surrounding shield.

The explosion sent bodies flying everywhere. When the dust settled, I got up and ran again. Beside me, his face appeared, first like a phantom just before he dropped the invisibility cloak from his body. The man was a genius.

We broke through the doors to find an empty entrance. I'd expected an army waiting for us, but there was no one but Kianna. We prepared to battle the woman, but she put up no fight. She rushed me and pulled me into a tight embrace.

"Thank you," she whispered in my ear. "There isn't much time, follow me."

She turned and headed away from us to the staircase that lead up to the second floor. Instead of climbing it, she moved along the side of it, touching the panels along it in strategic places before she made it to the back of the wall. The last panel popped open. We followed her, ducking inside of the opening before it sealed shut behind us.

"The seed is being kept down below. They knew you would return and had me move it."

"Why are you helping us?"

"I've read reports that I shouldn't have. The leaders of the Dark and the Light knew what was happening. They figured it out, and still they tried to stop this from happening. All those people, they don't know that you are doing this for us, but I do. And I thank you for your sacrifice." She continued to lead us down a tight corridor. "It won't be long until they figure out you're here and that I helped you."

"Thank you," Horacio spoke.

"It's right through there." She pointed to a heavy metal door.

"There is no handle, how do we get in?"

"I don't know. It was open the last time I was here. It closed shut behind me."

"Let me look." Horacio investigated the door.

"This is pointless," I huffed. "They'll figure out we're down here soon."

"You need to hurry," Kianna echoed my sentiment with an anxious look on her face.

"I'm trying."

I knelt beside him to look for a way to open the door. The palm of my hand rested on the surface and it vibrated. I hopped back, "Shit."

"What happened? Whats wrong?"

"You didn't feel that?"

"No, what was it?"

I placed my hand on the door again and again it vibrated. After a moment, the floor was vibrating too.

"What is that?" Kianna asked.

"It's a vibrational connection."

"A what?" I looked at Horacio, who offered the answer.

"The seed. I think you're connected to it. That's the difference in you now. Since you touched it, it's a part of you now."

"And it's vibrating the door?"

"If that vibration gets powerful enough," he didn't have time to finish his statement. The fissure spread across the height of the door. A moment later, the thick metal shattered.

The vibrations ended as my eyes found the seed suspended in the air in the middle of the room.

"They're coming!" Kianna yelled and in a flash of light, disappeared from the space.

"Guess that's as far as her support gets us." Horacio turned to me after staring at the empty spot where Kianna disappeared from.

"You can't expect her to put her neck on the line any more than she already has. Either way, I'm not getting out of this, and your chances are low for sticking by me."

"Yeah, I guess I've made a poor bet."

"Yeah, I guess so."

"We have to seal this place off."

"How?" I looked at the bag strapped over his shoulder. "Any more barrier spells in there?"

"No, I wish I had."

"Okay, so then the old-fashioned way." I stood in front of the doorway and held my hands out in front of me. Centering myself, I breathed through the magic. It would take everything I had, but what I had, I would no longer need when I was done.

The barrier formed from the ground up. It was slow going at first but I felt the vibration again, this time feeding my magic and the transparent barrier snapped into place. On the other side, the guards came into the view. They ran for the door and within moments began trying to break it down.

"We just have to keep them out long enough to finish this." I looked over my shoulder to Horacio.

"Well, the book said you'd have to ingest the Origin Seed and just wait for it to happen. How long could that take?" We both looked over to the suspended seed.

There was static in the air and then I saw them. The image of my mother and sister magically projected into the basement of the Hull.

"Mom, Camille?" I moved from the door.

"So, he's the hunk whose caused us all this trouble?" Camille sucked her teeth as she eyed Horacio.

"Hello," he responded nervously.

"You're doing this?" she asked me as the first strike of power hit the barrier at the door.

"Shit, they're going to get through." Horacio moved to the door and summoned what magic he could to keep the barrier up. Using his Light magic in the Dark territory was against the law, but we were far on the other side of that spectrum.

"Don't sacrifice yourself." The sound of my mother's sorrowful voice brought me back to her and my sister.

"I have to." I shifted closer to the image of my mother. "If you were here, I'd hug you. I'm sorry for everything. You know I have to do this."

"Yes, I know."

"What are you saying? Stop her?" Camille urged my mother. "We agreed that we wouldn't allow this."

"Camille, I love you, I do." The tears fell from my face. "This is so much bigger than me. I'm doing this for you. It may not seem like it now, but I hope like hell that one day you understand that. Mom will explain it to you if she hasn't already."

"My daughter," my mother's image faded and a moment later she was there. Not a projection. She was there with me, risking everything, and it meant everything to me. She pulled me into an embrace and sobbed. "I am so proud of you and I love you, and I am so sorry that you have the weight of such and impossible task on your shoulders."

"I can't hold this much longer!" Horacio called out.

"I have to do this mother." Camille's image still flickered next to us. "I love you both so much."

"I know you do." My mother moved away from me and tapped Horacio on the shoulder. She held her hands up, using her magic to hold the barrier, and spoke through tearful strength. "Go, be with her."

I stood by the seed as Horacio joined me. He pulled my hand into his and lifted it to his lips.

"It's time." A tear slid down my cheek. "I was foolish enough to think this would be easy. That ending my life would be some simple thing. Now, standing here, all I want to do is stretch out this moment. This should be easy, giving my life for a greater cause."

"I couldn't imagine this ever being a simple thing to do, Sierra. Your life is just as precious and as valuable as every other living thing on this planet."

"I'm scared," the laughter choked me. "I'm supposed to be a Daughter of the Dark. Fearless and unfeeling. This would have been much easier to do if I couldn't feel the fear."

"Do you think you'd be here if you couldn't feel?"

"Hell no." That time, the laughter filled the small room. "Okay, time to do this."

I plucked the seed from the air, once again feeling the connection to it. It spread over my body in a million minor explosions. I looked at Horacio once more for courage before I bit down into it. As the first bite slid down my throat, the rest of the remaining bit turned to ash and fell from my hand.

"That's it then." My empty hand hung between us.

"How do you feel?" Horacio placed his hands on my shoulders and gazed into my eyes.

"Strange, I'm not sure." My knees went weak, and I fell to the floor.

Horacio dropped beside me and pulled me into his arms. "I'm here."

"Stay with me?" I pleaded as the sounds of war carried on by the door.

"I promise." He kept his eyes trained on me.

"Say something, anything." I lifted my hand to touch his cheek.

"They say sometimes a soul is reborn." His eyes flooded with tears shook the timbre of his voice.

"Is that right?" The smile on my face was a weak one. My body was becoming numb, the waves of explosions faded, now centering in my chest. I couldn't be sure if it was the effect of the Origin Seed or if it was because of him.

He kissed my forehead. "What would you be if you could

decide?"

"A dragon," I responded softly.

"They're extinct," he laughed. "That's not a very good bet."

"Yes, but if you ever saw one again," my voice cracked as the explosions in my chest became a soft wave of tingles. The end was near, "you'd know that I got my wish."

I tasted the salt of his tears as he kissed me and held me as tightly as he could. Eventually, even that wasn't enough to keep me warm.

I felt the cold take over first.

It stretched across my body.

But still there even in the last moment...

I felt his love.

Epilogue

Three years passed since Sierra sacrificed herself.

Horacio stood in his home with Maleficent. The large paned windows gave him an unobstructed view of the dismantling of the border wall. More than the Conjurns' extended survival, Sierra's sacrifice changed the people of the Dark. The Dark Conjurns could experience emotions they never had before. That change lead to more mixed couplings. The Light and the Dark were no longer different, they were one. It took years to do, but the public had spoken and the wall came down.

He smiled. They still had a long way to go, but he felt in his heart that the progress that had made meant that Sierra's sacrifice was not in vain. He couldn't be with her, but it opened up so many possibilities for others.

Just as he was about to turn from the window, a piercing sound caught his attention. If not for viewing the spans of the wings and the streak of blue fire that ripped through the sky, he would have never believed that he'd heard the cry of a dragon.

He watches her fly straight at him, and a tear fell from his eye.

Maleficent moaned and rubbed the side of her belly against his leg.

"Yeah, that's our girl," he laughed a heartfelt sound as the dragon cried again.

The End

ENJOY THIS BOOK?
YOU CAN MAKE A BIG
DIFFERENCE!

Reviews are the most powerful tools in my arsenal when it comes to getting attention for my books. Much as I'd like to, I don't have the financial muscle of a New York publisher. I can't take-out full-page ads in the newspaper or put posters on the subway.

(Not yet, anyway).

But I do have something much more powerful and effective than that, and it's something that those publishers would kill to get their hands on.

A committed and loyal bunch of readers.

Honest reviews of my books help bring them to the attention of other readers.

If you've enjoyed this book, I would be very grateful if you could spend just five minutes leaving a review (it can be as short as you like) on the book's Amazon page.

THANK YOU SO MUCH!

ABOUT
THE
AUTHOR

Jessica Cage is a bestselling author from Chicago. She often bleeds elements of her home town into her work. You can find out more about her and her signature Caged Fantasies at www.jessicacage.com. You can connect with Jessica on all social media at @jcageauthor, on Facebook at www.facebook.com/jcageauthor and you should send her an email at jessica@jessicacage.com if the mood strikes you.

Printed in Great Britain
by Amazon

32565474R00066